THE ROTTING WITHIN

MATT KURTZ

GRINDHOUSE
PRESS

Also by Matt Kurtz

Kinfolk
Monkey's Box of Horrors - Tales of Terror: Vol. 1
Monkey's Bucket of Horrors - Tales of Terror: Vol. 2
Monkey's Butcher Block of Horrors - Tales of Terror: Vol. 3

Special thanks to
Carrie, Andy, Rachel, and Kris

PART I
THEN

ONE

AFTER THE CLOCK STRUCK MIDNIGHT and silence settled back over the inn, Shirley Moore slid out of bed and abandoned her husband and baby girl in the dead of night.

Her decision to do so occurred earlier that day, after the handsome stranger they were renting a room to discreetly asked if she wanted respite from her husband's alcoholism and abuse. The refined, older gentleman—who was passing through and only staying for a night—offered to take her away, show her beautiful sights, and introduce her to a new family who would love and respect her unconditionally.

Staring deep into his dark eyes, Shirley answered, "Yes, I'll go," before he even finished the invitation, then agreed to meet him later on the front lawn of the Sunrise Bed & Breakfast, the business she and her husband Jack owned and operated.

Moments after the final chime of the grandfather clock in the lobby, the twenty-four-year-old did as instructed and climbed out of bed, careful not to wake Jack.

Forgoing a packed bag, her wallet, and shoes, she passed Victoria's room without pausing to kiss her three-year-old goodbye. Shirley simply couldn't risk the man outside growing impatient and moving on without her.

1

Once at their rendezvous point, she accepted his outstretched hand, one tipped with long, sharp, manicured nails.

They embraced, turned away from the three-story house, and headed down the long gravel driveway, disappearing into the darkness.

TWO

FIFTEEN YEARS LATER, SHIRLEY RETURNED home.

Alone. Changed.

Refusing to resume the role of subservient housewife to an abusive husband, she took control of both her marriage and their business in a way she never dared before.

Regrettably, Victoria was gone, having run away just shy of her seventeenth birthday. Probably realizing there was nothing worth sticking around for except cleaning up the mess from an alcoholic father, the young lady left no contact information and was never heard from again.

Like their daughter, their business also vanished. A room hadn't been rented in years. The house itself fell into such neglect, their once loyal seasonals now sought vacation spots elsewhere.

And Jack? He was still a drunk, any bright light he once radiated during their courtship completely extinguished from his mind, body, and soul. What remained in his husk was something cold, bitter, and downright pathetic.

But none of it concerned Shirley. Not anymore.

She had a job to do. Get the house prepared and avoid all distractions, including, if need be, the man she was still legally married to.

~

The real blow to Jack's ego wasn't Shirley's failure to offer an apology or explain her whereabouts for well over a decade, but that she returned home a success, at least monetarily, while he had failed.

Her method of amassing such wealth remained a mystery. Although she had the money, she didn't flaunt it, except for the new Cadillac she arrived in.

Once home, Shirley informed Jack money wasn't an issue anymore. She gathered the past dues spread throughout the house, drove into town, and wired the funds to each collector, paying everything in full.

She returned with a bag of groceries and a trunk full of cleaning supplies. While she brought in the food to prepare their lunch, Jack fetched the supplies from the car and was told to decide which bedroom he'd be residing in, since she was reclaiming the master bedroom for herself. Between bites of their sandwiches, Shirley notified her husband the next step in the revival of their business was to restore and renovate the inn, expenses she'd cover as part of a future investment.

Jack felt emasculated about the whole situation . . . until seeing the big picture. Still married, half of her wealth was his, which meant he had money again. But he didn't know where she kept it. At least not yet.

Just shut up and smile and take her shit until you figure a way to get your hands on it.

Jack took any passive-aggressive jabs with a nod and a grin, dreaming of the moment he'd put her back in her place like the good ol' days. Until then, he'd have to bend over and take it a while.

Still, on those days when Shirley's arrogance shot into overdrive, he wished someone would put him out of his misery so he wouldn't have to listen to her bullshit anymore.

Then, a few weeks later, *they* arrived . . . and they were more than happy to grant him that wish.

THREE

THE UPPER LEVELS OF THE inn were dark. Vacant. Heavy rain pelted the roof.

Shirley sat in the living room rocker by the window, staring out like a dog waiting for its master. Jack was slumped in a chair slightly behind her, his thoughts drifting to the whiskey buried deep in the back of the bottom kitchen cabinet. He licked his lips and wondered how much longer it'd be before his wife went to bed so he could pay the bottle a visit.

While lightning strobed the dark woods and surrounding property, Shirley rambled about how, in order to make money, they'd have to spend it, hence all the remodeling for the last month and a half. She carried on about how good word of mouth was worth more than any newspaper or radio ad. And how it'd be only a matter of time before they were renting rooms again.

Then something beyond the window caught her eye. She leaned in so close her breath fogged the glass. "Why . . . here they are now."

Jack craned his neck to see around her. Whenever someone pulled up the driveway, the vehicle's headlights always swept the front windows of the house, yet he'd seen nothing.

Maybe lightning masked their approach.

Shirley sprung from her chair, pointed at him, and did a little dance. "I told you they'd come! I told you-I told you-I told you! You just have to have faith."

He was taken aback by her sudden change in demeanor. The stoic strength she returned home with slipped and gave way to a giddy brat. He had the overwhelming urge to bust her one across the chops to shut her up. What stopped him was her ghastly grin, like there were fishhooks piercing the corners of her mouth, with both sides pulled high by an invisible line. To slap her meant he'd have to touch her and that wasn't about to happen given her creepy-ass smile.

Already unnerved, the three loud knocks at the door made him jump.

"Ooooahhhhh." Shirley wiggled her fingers at him and laughed hysterically before floating away to greet the new arrivals.

Jack wondered if his wife had suddenly lost her marbles. He shifted to the edge of his seat and heard her open the front door. An inaudible conversation took place on the stoop. He strained to eavesdrop, even leaning out of his chair to glimpse the visitors, but the extended wall blocked his view.

Lightning flashed and a trio of shadows from the porch spilled across the lobby floor. Jack glanced down at the flickering silhouettes. From his vantage point, it looked like two adults and a . . .

A child?

He cocked his head. No. It was too big, too broad to be a kid. Even a fat one. Maybe a large dog? Like a rottweiler.

Or is that someone . . . crouching?

He brushed aside the absurd thought and went to see what kind of vehicle they arrived in. Finding the driveway empty, he slid to the window overlooking the porch. As he inched back the curtain, the front door slammed shut.

"This way, please," Shirley said from around the corner. "Let's get you checked in so you can change out of those wet clothes."

Jack moved to the lobby where a check-in desk had been added during the remodeling for an air of authenticity. He rounded the corner and saw two people standing opposite Shirley, now behind the counter. Both were garbed in long, dark, hooded rain slickers.

One of them shrugged off the jacket to reveal a woman in her mid-forties with shoulder length hair, a hard, masculine face, and piercing blue eyes. The other remained cloaked and kept their back to Jack. Based upon the small frame, hunched shoulders, and the bony, feminine fingers clutching a wooden cane, Jack figured it was another woman. An elderly one. For whatever reason, this Miss Mysterio appeared to be purposely concealing her face.

A suitcase, wooden trunk, and large wicker basket sat between them. It must've been the combo of those items that cast the odd shadow seen earlier across the lobby floor. Jack stepped closer to introduce himself and a floorboard creaked under his weight.

The hooded figure cocked her head at the noise but did not turn. Shirley and the other woman did.

"Ladies, this is my husband, Jack."

Jack's eyes darted to Shirley. Husband? Hell, that was the first time she acknowledged him as such since returning. About damn time. He puffed up a little and waved at the mannish woman with the icy blue eyes. The other, Miss Mysterio, kept her back to him, showing zero interest in introductions (not that it really bothered Jack any).

"Jack, can you take their belongings to rooms 3A and B while I check them in?"

The rooms were on the third floor, which also contained the attic entrance.

He glanced at the wooden trunk. Looked heavy. "Third floor? Got plenty of good rooms down here on the first. Why not give 'em a couple of those? That way they won't have to walk up and down two flights of stairs all the time." He gave the mannish one a wink and nod that read, *Just lookin' out for ya, ma'am.*

The woman stared blankly at him.

"I gave them the third floor," Shirley said, "because that's what they requested."

Miss Mannish with the blue eyes nodded. "We like our privacy."

Jack glanced around. "Well, shoot. You two are our only guests here. Can't get much more private than tha—"

"Jack!" Shirley snapped. "Would you just respect our guests' wishes and bring their belongings upstairs?"

He shot his wife a look. Since her return, he'd tolerated her taking that tone with him in private, but not now. Oh, hell no. Not with others around.

Shirley met his glare and ticked her head at the luggage. "Please." Her inflection was more command than polite request. She turned back to the guests.

"Now," she continued, softening her tone, "If you would sign our register, I can tell you about the amenities we have to offer."

Jack huffed and went to retrieve the luggage. When he stepped up beside the old woman with the cane, she growled and turned further away.

He gave her an incredulous look, snorted, and grabbed the wicker basket, which stunk like a wet dog.

Jack lifted it, rising so fast he nearly fell backwards. Given its size and bulk, he assumed it would have some weight, but the damn thing was empty. "Lil' warning would've been nice," he mumbled under his breath.

On a positive note, the basket and suitcase could now be combined to make one less trip. He grabbed the bag and stacked it on top of the basket and carried both upstairs. Reaching the second-floor landing, he glanced down at the lobby, hoping the old bat had shrugged off her jacket so he could finally see her face.

No such luck. The coat remained on, and hood up.

Whatever, lady, he thought while trudging down the hall to the next flight of stairs around the corner.

Something about those two ruffled his feathers. Or was it Shirley? It sure seemed like she was showing off in front of them, bossing him around like that.

More puzzling was how the women arrived. There was no vehicle in the driveway or parked in the side lot. From the main road, the inn's driveway was nearly a mile stretch through woods and dense foliage. Such isolation was a deciding factor when buying the place using Shirley's inheritance from a rich aunt. So if a cab had dropped them off, Jack should've seen its headlights at some point. Or heard an engine. Or a door or trunk slam shut.

Thunder and lightning must've concealed it because the alternative meant the two old women simply stepped out of the cold, dark woods.

FOUR

THE WOMEN WERE THERE A little over a week and rarely left the confines of 3A or B, the only rooms on that floor. Myrna, the blue eyed one, was spotted downstairs upon occasion, but the other, Lucille, the one with the cane, had yet to show her face. Much like an old cat, she slunk around only at night while everyone else slept. On occasion, Jack would hear the thump of a cane and catch a shadow pass by the strip of hall light under his door, but he refused to peek out or give chase for a proper introduction. He told himself it had less to do with fear and more about not giving a fat turd about her bony ass.

As creepy as the women were, Jack considered them a blessing since Shirley's every waking moment was spent waiting on them hand and foot, overcompensating with her hospitality. Maybe it was because all that money she spent remodeling only attracted two guests and she was too proud to admit her gamble hadn't paid off.

In any case, with Shirley so occupied, it gave Jack more opportunities to sneak away and spend a little quality time with the bottle.

~

His last night alive was a cold December evening. Jack was looking for a little something to nip the chill from his bones. With everyone asleep and Lucille having already made her midnight rounds, he retrieved a bottle of Evan Williams from the kitchen cabinet and turned it up for a much-needed swig.

Its warmth lit him up, both mind and spirit. It was ridiculous resorting to such shenanigans, a grown man essentially stealing from the cookie jar behind mama's back, but he'd already depleted his stash upstairs and his thirst demanded quenching. Three pulls on the bottle later, he noticed the memo under the refrigerator magnet. He lowered the whiskey, hissed at its delicious burn, and narrowed his eyes to read in the dark.

Jack,
Bring in more firewood for the bin (ASAP) before it rains.
—S

Oh shit! He'd seen the note earlier that day but forgotten about it since. He leaned over and stared out the kitchen window. Everything was wet and reflecting silver light from the full moon above.

Well, ya dummy. Now you're really gonna get an earful in the morning.

It was best to fetch the wood anyway and leave it in the porch bin. If it were still wet in the morning, he could blame it on the dampness in the air instead of his forgetfulness.

After another swig to keep his belly warm, he shrugged on his jacket and stepped out onto the covered porch. The reserve pile sat across the yard by the tree line, kept at a distance to prevent termites and other critters from invading the inn.

Jack walked to the edge of the porch and clicked on his flashlight. The mist danced in its beam. Letting off a hearty shiver, he started across the yard, his feet sliding through the wet grass and breath visible in the frigid air.

Stacked in the far corner of the lot, the pile ran at a ninety-degree angle. It was roughly twenty feet long, one row deep, and stood at a height equal to Jack's shoulders. The top tier was wet and useless but the wood below was good to go. Jack set the flashlight on the opposite row running perpendicular and aimed it back in his direction as a work light. He slid over a few logs from the top, cherry-picked the rows underneath, and gathered an armful of wood.

A musky scent rode the incoming breeze. Then a twig snapped somewhere behind the pile.

Jack froze. *Probably just a raccoon or possum. Or, shit . . . coyote.* He craned his neck to peer over the pile.

The undergrowth behind it crunched and something skittered closer.

With his arms full of firewood, Jack quickly backpedaled to a safer distance and came to a stop.

An eerie chitter rose from the other side. There was a blur of motion at the opening he'd made in the stack.

Then movement at the flashlight caught his eye.

A huge spider-like thing crawled up from behind the woodpile. It moved toward the light but stopped short of entering its beam. Jack could see its body was roughly the size of a softball by the way the moon reflected off its dark, slick surface. Its long, spindly appendages reminded him of the king crab legs served at the fancy lobster place in town, only these were jet black instead of orange.

The critter was huge but, unless it had wings, Jack felt confident he was keeping a safe enough distance. Still, he dropped the armful of wood, all except for a thinner piece to use as a club.

In response to his action, the thing scuttled over and straddled the flashlight.

Jack waited to see what it was going to do next. They remained locked in some sort of standoff for a good minute.

Okay, enough bullshit. It was time to reclaim his property before the batteries went dead. Raising the stick, he stepped closer and the spider-thing crouched as if ready to pounce.

Jack halted and gripped his makeshift club white-knuckle tight. *Okay. So this is how you wanna play, huh?* If he moved fast enough and swung sideways, he could bat it off the light. Swing for the fences and knock the sucker straight out of the ballpark.

As if reading his intentions, the thing clamped down onto the flashlight, the action making an unnerving clacking sound as its long legs entwined the aluminum shaft.

The flashlight spun in Jack's direction and blasted his face.

He shielded his eyes with his hand and peeked out between splayed fingers. Before he could utter "What the fuuuuu . . ." the light clicked off.

Jack slowly lowered his arm and waited for his eyes to re-adjust to the dark.

A maniacal laugh made the hairs along his neck stand up.

From out of the gloom, a tall, thin, humanoid figure—still clutching the flashlight—slowly rose from behind the woodpile.

Jack's jaw unhinged over the realization it wasn't a spider he'd been staring at, but an enormous hand, one with long quadruple-jointed fingers.

The dark entity tossed aside the flashlight and whispered, "*Jaaaaack . . .*"

With a hammering heart, Jack spun and made a mad dash for the house.

Behind him, the wood pile exploded, followed by heavy steps in hot pursuit.

Jack threw a glance back and let off a shrill scream as the tall figure dropped to all fours, galloping on lean, muscular limbs. Completely naked, its flesh was jet black, as if dipped in tar. The hot breath it exhaled in the frigid air masked its face, except for two yellowish-orange eyes burning like hellfire through the haze. It snorted, panted, and picked up its pace.

Bounding up the porch steps, Jack ripped open the backdoor, pivoted on his heels, and was about to pull it shut when he glimpsed the horrific face barreling out of the dark toward him. First, he saw those burning eyes, and then a huge maw of razor-sharp teeth.

Jack shrieked at the visage and pulled on the door with all his might. Before it could seal shut, a clawed hand shot through the quickly narrowing gap, grabbed hold of the door, and stopped it dead. Jack pulled harder, but it refused to budge. Instead, the backdoor slowly began to open, dragging him forward as his wet heels squeaked and sought traction, leaving scuff marks across the polished linoleum floor. Jack already pissed himself before reaching the porch, now his bowels cramped and felt like they were about to release and run down the back of his legs. The doorknob, slick with his sweat, was either going to slip from his grasp or snap off its plate.

Jack squealed and searched for a possible escape route.

There was the large laundry room connected to the kitchen, but the door had no lock. The nearest room that did was Shirley's and it was halfway across the house. He'd never make it there once letting go of the handle.

"Shirley!" he screamed over his shoulder. "My shotgun! Get my shotgun!"

No reply.

"Shirley! Wake up! Goddammit! Help me! Help me!"

He lost a little more slack on the door. Even if she had heard him, she'd never retrieve the gun in time. Barricading himself in the laundry room was his only option. He could put a washer or dryer between him and the beast, using it to block the door and prevent it from being pushed open. Then he'd continue screaming for help and hope Shirley pulled her head out of her ass long enough to hear his cries and call the sheriff.

The back door slid open a few more inches.

Needing a new strategy, Jack thought to do the unexpected: shove the door *open* so it would slam into the thing and, hopefully, throw it off balance, at least long enough to give him a head start for the laundry room.

He reversed his action and pushed as hard as he could.

The door flew forward and hit its target. The beast let off a grunt of surprise and stumbled back.

Jack rushed for the laundry room and heard the porch door rip open. Wood cracked and glass shattered behind him. Ignoring the commotion, he focused solely on the closed laundry door ahead. He wrenched its handle and shoved, but the door didn't budge. He screamed. Tried again. Then remembered . . .

It opened *outward*, not in.

"Oh, shit." So much for barricading himself inside.

He ripped open the door and the beast tackled him from behind. The violent blow blasted the air from his lungs and propelled him into the dark laundry room, where he bellyflopped onto the floor and was sandwiched between hard linoleum and the crushing weight of the creature straddling his back. His ribs flexed, bent inward, and snapped with a sharp crack. A torturous pain exploded across his chest.

The thing flipped him onto his back, making Jack face his attacker.

Through tear-filled eyes, he saw only a blurry, elongated silhouette against the harsh kitchen light. He strained and threw a weak punch, but the creature easily caught it, clamping its long fingers over his fist, and forcefully squeezed. As Jack squealed, the bones in his clenched hand splintered and everything above the wrist compressed into a crimson pulp. Groaning in agony, he feebly slapped at his assailant with his good hand. The beast snatched it and effortlessly snapped it all the way back, breaking his wrist.

Jack went bug-eyed and howled in pain.

The creature yanked up Jack's mangled hands and inspected the damaged instruments once used to abuse Shirley for so many years. It grunted in satisfaction and released its grip, letting Jack's limp arms fall back to his side.

"Please . . ." Jack whispered through gritted teeth. Pain sucked out what little air remained in his lungs. He watched in horror as the creature's hand rose over its shoulder, winding up for a killing blow. "*No! Plea—*"

The beast swung. Its strike to the chin let off a sickening crack, dislocating Jack's jaw at a forty-five-degree angle. The bone tore through his cheek, bisecting it into meaty petals. His tongue bounced through the hemorrhaging wound as if attached to a spring. In a gurgling hiss, the lower half of his face deflated and became horribly disfigured.

The creature struck again and again. With each powerful swipe, razor-sharp talons sliced through tender flesh and, in the final phase of remodeling the inn, painted the laundry room red with Jack's blood.

PART II
NOW

FIVE

TWENTY-SIX YEARS LATER

KENZIE SAT CURBSIDE BEHIND THE wheel of her Jeep Cherokee and waited for the kids to spill onto the sidewalk. Although it was early April and warm enough for shorts and a t-shirt, she wore long sleeves and jeans to hide the bruises.

She checked the side-mirrors and rearview, barely able to see over the boxes and trash bags stuffed with their belongings in the back.

The clock on the dash read three-sixteen. Only four more minutes until the bell sounded. She tapped the steering wheel and looked back at the main doors of the elementary school. She eyed the exit lane to her left to make sure it was still clear. That open lane would be their lifeline if a white F-150 pick-up were to suddenly approach from the rear.

Now a bundle of nerves, she checked her surroundings again and exhaled, her left leg bouncing like a jackhammer. *Relax. He's at work. This is gonna go just fine.*

Kenzie took a slow, calming breath.

But what if he goes home early? He'll know the minute he sees the apartment. And this'll be the first place he'll come.

All three mirrors were rechecked.

The clock on the dash clicked to three-nineteen.

Almost there.

She glanced down at the track phone secretly purchased a week ago after fearing he might've installed a tracking app on her old cell. They used stuff like that in movies all the time and she didn't know how much of it was bullshit, but Kenzie couldn't risk it, so she left the old phone on their bed back at the apartment. Besides, if she had kept it, he'd call that number nonstop, expecting her to pick up. She didn't need that constant ringing reminder of him or to hear his threatening messages. She was done. It was over. And it was the only way to leave someone like him behind.

When the school bell finally rang, she fired up the engine, raring to go. The doors to the building swung open and, much like an anthill being kicked, the children swarmed the school yard. A few minutes later, Lilly and her five-year-old half-brother Tim separated from the crowd, spotted their mom, and made a beeline for the SUV.

Kenzie popped the locks and they climbed in back.

"Whoa. What's all this?" Tim asked, motioning to the packed cargo area.

"Come on, guys. Strap in, so we can talk."

Once securing them in their seats, Kenzie pulled into the exit lane.

"Well?" Tim asked.

Kenzie knew it was best to tell the truth, but still paused before speaking. "It's all our stuff. We're going away. On a secret trip."

"What's going on, Mom?" Lilly asked.

Kenzie heard the uneasiness in the nine-year-old's voice and smiled to reassure her things were fine. "We're gonna go see someone. Stay with them for a while."

"Who?" Tim asked, excited.

"Great-Grandma."

"Wha?" Tim said. "Grandma's in heaven."

"No, not *Grandma* Grandma." Kenzie made sure to bump up the enthusiasm in her voice, hoping it would be contagious. "*Great-*Grandma. Great-Grandma Shirley."

"If she's so great," Lilly said, "how come we've never heard of her before?"

Tim raised his hand. "Wait, is this Dad's mom?"

"Whose dad?" Lilly asked him. "Yours or mine?"

Both kids looked at each other in confusion and turned to their mother for the answer.

Kenzie exhaled. "Neither. She's my mom's mother."

"Grandma's mom?"

Kenzie had to think for a moment. "Ummm, yeah. . . *yes!* Yes, Grandma's mom. *My* maternal grandmother. And your great-grandma."

Lilly eyed their belongings in back. "Ma, if this is all our stuff, please tell me you grabbed my books."

"Of course, honey. But you have so many. I could only grab a few."

"From where?"

"Off your desk."

"But from which side? The right side is stuff I already read. And the left is my *to-be*-read. Please tell me you grabbed the pile on the left. Please!"

"I—I think it was."

"Maaaa?! You *think?*"

"What about Paul?" Tim blurted.

The mere mention of his name dropped the temperature a few degrees and the vehicle fell silent.

"Yeah," Lilly asked after a moment. "Is he coming too?"

Both kids waited with bated breath. Kenzie knew the answer they were hoping for and it broke her heart, proving she'd exposed them to a toxic environment. "No. This is only for us. Our family."

"Paul won't like it," Tim whispered.

Kenzie looked at her children in the rearview mirror. "That doesn't matter anymore. So don't you worry about Paul." She made sure the last statement came out beaming with confidence . . . although she completely lacked it. "Now who wants to go meet Great-Grandma Shirley?"

"Is she nice?"

"Does she have white hair?"

Kenzie shrugged. She'd only spoken to the old woman for the first time a few days ago. And as for the answers to their questions, "Yes and probably. Now let's hit the road. Later we can stop at McDonald's for Happy Meals and sundaes. You guys okay with that?"

Tim and Lilly cheered their approval and broke out giggling.

God, Kenzie loved the sound of their laughter. It was almost alien to her.

"All right. Let's go meet Great-Grandma Shirley."

She checked her mirrors once more and focused on the road ahead.

SIX

A SIMPLE GLANCE, LINGERING A few seconds too long, made Kenzie realize she had to leave Paul immediately.

She always told both kids to keep the bathroom door closed and locked when using it. The same went for the bedroom whenever they were getting dressed. She explained, although Paul was an adult, he had no business being around when either action was taking place. Of course, she made sure to phrase it both casually yet firmly, partially out of not wanting to freak them out, but also in case they inadvertently repeated her warning to him. After all, they were kids, who most times had no filter. If Paul did find out, he would not be happy about its insinuation. Not at all.

Then one morning before school, Lilly—fresh out of the shower, her hair wet and wearing only a towel—pranced into the apartment living room to fetch something from her backpack. Kenzie was in the kitchen making breakfast when her daughter entered, passing Paul, who was on the recliner watching the morning news. Seeing how Lilly's hair was possibly wet enough to drip onto the carpet, Kenzie's first instinct was to check if Paul was angry. If he appeared the least bit upset, she wanted to scold the girl before he could say anything. Not only would it spare her daughter Paul's sharp tongue, but make Kenzie look like she had a firm grip over her kids. It was sad she thought that way but, in the past, Paul took a sadistic pleasure in showing Kenzie what happens to mommies who can't control their brats (of which his favorite method of punishment caused her to bleed rectally for days afterwards).

Before she could reprimand her daughter about the wet hair, Kenzie witnessed Paul leering at the child while bent over digging through her backpack.

His eyes crawled over every inch of her body. And when he licked his lips, Kenzie's stomach twisted so sharply she almost gasped.

"Lilly!" Kenzie said, louder than intended.

Paul jolted over the outburst and quickly turned back to the television.

"You're dripping all over the carpet! Hurry and get to your room and get dressed for school. Now!"

As the child left, Kenzie continued watching Paul to see if he'd sneak a peek at the little girl again. Instead, his eyes slid over and locked on Kenzie and she quickly looked away to avoid antagonizing him.

With the scene replaying in her head, Kenzie gripped the steering wheel tight, checked her rearview mirror again, and took a deep breath.

The repulsive incident was the catalyst to get out before anything happened to her babies. From the start, she'd taken Paul's abuse, both physically and mentally. She'd made excuses for him and tried to shield the kids from it, but they must've heard the arguments from the other room and, sometimes, her cries. The episode with Lilly only foreshadowed the next level of abuse.

Fight or flight? Her options were limited. She had no savings, with her entry-level job as an administrative assistant barely covering her half of the bills. Any friends she once had were long gone, losing touch or burning bridges with them at the demand of whichever control freak she was dating at the time. Having never known her father and after her mother's death from breast cancer at the young age of forty-three, Kenzie had no family. With Lilly's dad in prison and Tim's father penniless from the family he started after he and Kenzie broke up, it was pointless to ask either for help. Staying at a shelter was an option, but only a final one because of the kids.

Then out of the blue, she remembered her mother, Victoria, talking about growing up with her shitty-ass father, Jack, Kenzie's grandfather. Feeling robbed of a family history, Kenzie relished any stories about her grandparents, on those rare occasions her mom spoke of them. Victoria recalled nothing of her mother since the woman abandoned them when she was a baby. However, she did mention they owned a bed and breakfast outside of Penumbra, Texas, in case Kenzie ever wanted to make the trek back to meet her granddaddy . . . that is, if the man hadn't already drank himself to death. Victoria warned Kenzie not to expect much, and how she'd probably be disappointed at what she'd find, but still wanted to throw the option out there. Such a glowing endorsement gave Kenzie little incentive to make the journey. She usually had more than enough negativity in her life. Why add to it?

But now, with her back against the wall, it might be worth it, at the very least, to make a phone call. Searching online at work, she narrowed the possibilities to a few inns. It took her a couple of days to gather the courage, and when she finally dialed the numbers, it was the third one on the list that caused her racing heart to skip a beat.

A soft-spoken woman answered the phone and Kenzie asked if the owners had a daughter named Victoria Moore.

There was a long pause.

"Why, yes. We do." Then a gasp on the other end. "Oh, my God . . . Oh, my God, Victoria? Is it you?"

Suddenly, Kenzie was equally caught off guard. She had no idea she'd been talking to her own grandmother and how the woman had apparently returned home.

"No-no-no. I'm sorry. But this is her daughter, Kenzie."

It must have been bittersweet for the old woman to find out she had a granddaughter and great grandkids, but that her own daughter had passed away years ago. Once Shirley got over the initial shock from the unexpected call and the news it brought, the woman invited Kenzie and the kids for a visit.

In fact, she insisted on it. And the sooner, the better.

Kenzie gushed in relief. Thank God, now they had somewhere to go to get away from Paul, even if it was temporary. She'd take it one day at a time and feel things out. Although Shirley was blood, they were still strangers to one another, and Kenzie didn't want to impose on the woman too much. But she'd catch one hell of a break if they all clicked, and she and the kids were invited to stay long enough for Kenzie to get back on her feet.

~

It would take quite a bit of gas money traveling to Texas, especially with their destination located near its southern border. Even if her credit cards weren't maxed out, any charges would leave a paper trail. What Kenzie needed was cash. Her solution lay hidden in the back of Paul's dresser. Whether he was nostalgic or fashionably challenged, he kept a fanny pack there, stuffed with a few hundred dollars. Kenzie never asked what the money was for, since the first thing out of his mouth would be, *How do you know about that? And why the fuck are you snooping through my shit?*

The money would definitely get them there, but not much farther.

Considering her boyfriend once gave her a beating for forgetting about wet clothes left in the washer from the night before, stealing money from him might not be the wisest decision. But if that's what it took to get them out of there, then the risk was worth it.

So, she did something stupid. Something that might guarantee his pursuit.

Kenzie checked the rearview again for headlights. The highway behind her was dark. They were alone.

And for the first time in a long time, that felt incredible.

SEVEN

THE TREES ENCLOSING THE GRAVEL driveway were like entwined arthritic fingers, their dense foliage strangling the noon sun. Kenzie carefully maneuvered the Jeep along the path, her eyes scanning for signs of civilization. The directions dictated to her over the phone by Shirley sat on the passenger seat. Initially dismissing them as antiquated in the age of GPS and Google Maps, she was grateful to have them after her cell signal went dead approaching the signs for Penumbra, TX. The sudden signal loss was chalked up to the cheap burner phone, getting exactly what she paid for.

"Are we lost?" Lilly asked.

Kenzie jumped. She thought the girl was asleep but a quick check in the rearview showed Lilly rubbing her eyes and yawning. Her brother still napped in the seat beside her. "I don't think so, honey. This is the way Great-Grandma said to go."

Although Shirley gave her a back-road shortcut that avoided the town altogether and shaved a half hour off her trip, she would've preferred to know where civilization lay in case they needed to turn around. On a positive note, they'd hit all the natural landmarks she was told to watch for, so they had to be on the right track.

Lilly unbuckled her seatbelt and leaned forward, resting her head against her mother's shoulder for a better view out the windshield.

"Dunno, Mom. Looks like we should turn around."

"Well, Great-Grandma Shirley said it was out in the boonies, so I think we're still okay."

"Why does she live way out here in the woods?"

"Probably so the people coming here feel like they're far away from all the usual craziness in their lives."

"But why the woods?"

"For a change of scenery. And for peace and quiet, I guess. To be one with nature."

"Huh?"

"It's like going camping. Only in a way Mommy prefers to do it. With air conditioning, indoor plumbing, and screens on all the windows and doors to keep out the bugs.

"Is there gonna be a lot of people here?"

"Don't know, hon. Guess we'll find out. That is, whenever we . . . oh, wait. Lookee here."

A sign for the Sunrise Bed & Breakfast was nestled within some brush. Then the inn appeared around the bend. The three story, nineteenth-century Victorian home sat in a large clearing. Both the house and its property were well kept. Although the place was huge, it remained cozy and inviting.

Lilly's eyes expanded. "Wow. Is this our new home?"

Kenzie chuckled. "No. We're only visiting." She knew better than to say any more since a kid's honesty-meter ran extremely high and lacked discretion. The last thing she needed was them blurting to Shirley they were homeless and looking for a place to stay. *Not that I wouldn't mind crashing here for a while*, she thought.

Wiping the sleep from his eyes, Tim came up behind Lilly and hooked his chin over her shoulder. "We there yet?"

A rectangular lot designated as guest parking sat just off the driveway, near the tree line. The area was empty. In fact, unless a car was parked out back, there were no other vehicles around. The place appeared deserted, which meant plenty of vacant rooms. Kenzie couldn't help but smile since it also meant their visit wouldn't be too much of an imposition.

"Whoa. Is Great-Grandma rich?" Tim asked, obviously referring to the size of the house.

"Don't know," Kenzie answered. "This isn't only her home, it's her business. She rents rooms here. For vacations and stuff."

The Jeep Cherokee pulled into a shaded spot provided by

overhanging trees. Kenzie and the children climbed out and stretched after being on the road for three days. They'd broken up the trip with overnights at cheap motels, but she'd been driving since dawn, having to bribe the kids with pancakes to get them up extra early and on the road. Knowing there was at least another six hours of drive time, she wanted to make sure they reached the inn well before nightfall, considering how isolated the place was. The last thing she needed was to be driving around out there in the dark.

Now that they had arrived, her heart was racing. She wanted to blame it on the thermos of coffee chugged earlier and not on meeting her grandmother for the first time. Or the grave importance of impressing the old woman enough she'd ask them to stay longer than the few days they'd planned. Because this was it. She had no back-up plan. No money. No answers for the kids if they asked "Where are we gonna go? What are we gonna do?" once their visit concluded.

It's gonna be okay, she tried to tell herself. *It'll all work out. It's got to.* She quickly wiped her sweaty palms on her pant leg to avoid grossing out anyone willing to shake her hand.

"Tim, lock the doors on your side." Sure, they were out in the country and no one appeared to be around for miles, but the Jeep contained all their belongings. Better safe than sorry.

While Kenzie and Tim secured the SUV, Lilly walked to the rear of the vehicle and gave the house the once over. Her eyes stopped on a third-story window, its curtains drawn.

As if on cue, the seam split and one side pulled back a few inches, just enough for someone to peek out.

The awkward moment stretched far too long and whoever was watching wasn't just taking a casual glance. They were studying the new arrivals.

Lilly shivered. "Mom?" she said, her eyes still glued to the window.

Kenzie turned to her daughter as the front door to the house creaked open.

Lilly shifted her gaze down to the plump woman with gray hair stepping out onto the porch, then back up to the window where its curtain slowly dropped into place.

Kenzie slammed the car door, slung her purse over her shoulder, and wiped her palms on her pant leg again. If her heart was racing before, now it was damn near breaking the sound barrier.

The old woman waved from the edge of the porch and descended the steps.

While Kenzie and Tim returned the gesture, Lilly was occupied with the third-floor window, hoping to catch sight of whomever was spying on them.

Kenzie took a deep breath, stepped between the kids, and laid a reassuring hand on their shoulders. "C'mon," she said, guiding them forward. "And make sure to smile."

As they approached, Kenzie got a better look at the old woman. If this was indeed Shirley, she lived up to the image Kenzie conjured while first speaking to her over the phone. She was the textbook version of a grandmother, like one who loved to knit and bake cookies. Hell, even the small, round glasses she wore were perched on the edge of her plum-like nose.

They met halfway and the gray-haired woman was all smiles, practically gushing. Her stare shifted between Kenzie and the two children.

"Ohhhhh . . . would you look at these precious little angels?" she said. "Aren't they just perfect?"

"Shirley?" Kenzie said. Obviously, it was her, but a little confirmation would've been nice. Who knows? Maybe it was some overly friendly guest strolling the premises.

The woman nodded and reached for Kenzie's hands, clasping them together. Shirley's wrinkled palms were as soft as tissue paper and Kenzie hoped hers weren't still clammy.

"Oh, Kenzie. My word! Aren't you the most beautiful thing?"

Kenzie blushed, guffawed, and almost snorted. It had been a long time since anyone called her *that*. "Thank you."

The woman stepped closer, into Kenzie's personal space. There was no hug. No kiss on the cheek. Only Shirley's intense stare while wearing a huge-ass grin.

Kenzie let off a nervous giggle.

Shirley closed her eyes, slowly inhaled, and after a few uncomfortable moments, resumed her stare. The exchange immediately crossed from awkward to downright creepy.

Noticing Kenzie's uneasiness, Shirley stepped back and said, "It really is *so* nice to meet you, dear." She dropped Kenzie's hands and her attention fell to the children. "And who are these angels sent to us from Heaven?"

Kenzie answered, "This is Tim. And Lilly." She placed her hands on their shoulders again and gently squeezed. "Guys, say hello to your

Great-Grandma Shirley."

Both children shyly did as they were told.

Shirley hunched over, leaning on her thick thighs to meet them at eye level. "Oh, please! Call me Shirley. I don't need to be reminded of how old I am with this great-grandma business." Rising, she groaned and rubbed her lower back. "See what I mean? Besides, that's a title I must earn. Let's take things one day at a time, shall we?"

Kenzie nodded and the kids looked around the property, still taking in their new surroundings.

"Why don't we go inside, and I'll whip up some lunch. I hope sandwiches are okay?"

"I want a yellow cheese and bologna sammich," Tim said.

Kenzie patted his shoulder. "Let's see what Shirley has first before you start making demands, kiddo." Slightly embarrassed, she shrugged at Shirley, who dismissed the whole thing with a smile and wave of her hand.

As they made their way to the porch, Lilly hung back, stopping to give the third-floor window one last look. Finding the curtains slightly separated again, enough for someone to be watching from within the sliver of darkness, she gasped and bolted ahead, quickly catching up with her group.

EIGHT

THE FOOD AND DINNERWARE WERE nicer than what was served at their last Thanksgiving meal. Expensive looking plates, crystal-like glasses, and polished silverware were set before them. Cold cuts and cheese (including, much to Tim's satisfaction, bologna and American slices) were fanned across a silver platter. Every bread imaginable—from white, wheat, and rye to pumpernickel and Hawaiian rolls—filled a large basket. There were huge bowls of macaroni and potato salad alongside a baked mac and cheese casserole, its crunchy top layer of cheddar breadcrumbs still steaming.

Throughout the meal, Kenzie was terrified the kids would spill, break, or stain something. Lunch would've been so much more relaxing if only they were using plasticware and paper plates. Still, except for the few times Tim went for his drink and dropped the heavy fork onto his plate with a loud clank, the kids did good. They also kept their promise about not mentioning Paul to Shirley, which wasn't hard to do since they didn't like talking about him anyway.

The lunchtime conversation was kept light: which city they lived in, what the kids' interests were, what Kenzie did for a living, what they liked to do for fun. Shirley was all smiles except when she saw the bruises on Kenzie's arm as the young woman rolled up her sleeves at the table. The once purple handprint on her forearm was now fading to a dull yellow. Shirley handled the matter tactfully by remaining silent and throwing her attention back on the children.

After the meal, Tim and Lilly asked to be excused to go exploring out back.

"Now that's an excellent idea," Shirley said. "Go work up an appetite for dessert!"

The kids sprung from their seats.

"But please stay in the yard and away from the woodpile."

"Why?" Tim said. "Wassamatter with the woodpile?"

Shirley paused, then scrunched up her face like a comedic witch and wiggled her fingers at the boy. "'Cause, my pretties, it's filled with all sorts of snakes, spiders, and critters. Things that scuttle and slither and would love to . . ." she playfully poked above his belly. "Eat at your liver."

Tim giggled nervously and stepped back. "Really?"

Shirley dropped the act. "Well . . . yeah, actually. This is the country, so it's really nothing out of the norm. Just be careful where you play and always look where you're about to step whenever in high grass"

The kids suddenly seemed less enthusiastic about going out back.

Shirley noticed their reluctance. "If you prefer, you can stay on the porch. There's a toy box out there full of goodies we keep for our younger guests."

"Go on, guys," Kenzie said. "Stay out of the woods and away from the woodpile like Shirley said. And look out for each other. Okay?"

Tim grabbed Lilly's arm and pulled her out of the room. They stomped across the floor, rattling the silverware left on the plates. Kenzie would have to tell them later to tread much lighter to avoid making such a racket.

The back door opened and slammed shut.

Kenzie gave an uneasy look. "They'll be okay out there, right?"

Shirley patted her hand. "They'll be fine."

~

Standing on the edge of the porch, Tim and Lilly scoped out the backyard. The woodpile they'd been warned about—now a quarter of its size the night their Great-Grandpa Jack was eaten alive by whatever crawled out of it—was still located on the far side of the lot, near the tree line. With it being Spring, the pile wouldn't be replenished until late October, at the earliest.

Tim eyed the dense woods out back while Lilly went for the toy box, a weathered wooden crate sitting between two rusted folding chairs. It didn't appear promising, but she was curious about its contents.

She flipped the lid and something shot out, buzzing past her ear. The girl shrieked and swatted it away. By the time she pivoted to see what it was, it had already flown off the porch.

"What was *that*?" Tim said, eyes bulging. He was squatting with his arms shielding his head.

"Think it was just a big bumblebee." She extended a hand to help her little brother up. "C'mon. Let's check out what toys they got."

They went to the chest and peered inside. There was a deflated football, its skin flaked and rotting. A doll sewn out of an old sock with yarn for hair and missing one button eye. A crushed Tonka truck that wouldn't roll. One tennis racket, minus strings. An empty, rusted coffee can. And a single flip-flop with mold growing in the shape of a footprint.

"Yuck," Tim said.

Lilly dropped the lid and wiped her hands on her shorts. "Yeah. So how 'bout we go check out that wood pile?"

~

Out of the numerous framed photos decorating the buffet base, Kenzie selected one of her grandfather. Jack was at the lake, proudly showing off a large fish he'd caught. He looked happy. Healthy. Must have been before the booze completely consumed him.

"He had a nice smile," she said, feeling obligated to comment.

Shirley sat at the dining room table studying her own set of pictures, about a half dozen photographs of the daughter she never saw grow up to become a mother herself. Kenzie selected pictures of Victoria in her prime, before she got sick, when she was happy and healthy. They were duplicates Kenzie planned to give the old woman. Shirley glanced up from the photos. "Huh?"

Kenzie raised the framed photo of Jack at the lake. "His smile. It's nice."

Shirley shook her head almost in confusion as if to say *Why are you even talking to me about* him? "Oh. Yeah." Then she returned to the pictures of her daughter.

Kenzie gave her grandfather's photo one last look and set it down. During their initial phone conversation, she asked about Jack, if they'd be meeting him also. Shirley told her he passed away long ago.

Before Kenzie could offer her condolences, the old woman oddly added, "Animal attack. Brutal. Very messy." Then quickly changed the subject. There was definitely more to the story, but she accepted the bullet point version for now. She kept it even simpler when relaying the info to Lilly and Tim, only telling them Great-Grandpa Jack was no longer alive.

She sat beside Shirley and noticed the woman studying a head and shoulders shot of Victoria, the only real close-up picture in the bunch.

"She was beautiful," Shirley whispered.

"Yeah. She was."

Her eyes glassy, Shirley slowly looked over at Kenzie. "Did . . . did she suffer?"

Yes. Immensely.

Kenzie slowly inhaled and shook her head. "It took her fast." Then she broke eye contact. "And I was there when she went, so she wasn't alone at the end."

A tear rolled down Shirley's cheek. She wiped it away, sniffled, and patted Kenzie's hand. "Thank you for that."

After gathering the pictures of her deceased daughter, Shirley slid the stack to the center of the table, folded her hands in front of her, and smiled. It was an odd reaction, but Kenzie figured she'd return to the photos later in private.

They sat in a heavy silence until Kenzie cleared her throat. It was time to address the elephant in the room. "Look, Shirley. I wanna say I feel bad about not looking you guys up earlier. I mean, waiting this long to do so."

"Nonsense. I'm just as guilty. If not more so. But that's the past. What matters now is I've been blessed to meet you and my wonderful great-grandchildren."

Kenzie nodded in agreement and took a sip of coffee.

"What's important to me," Shirley continued, "is that we take this opportunity to catch up on lost time." She paused and squirmed slightly in her chair. "Now, I'd like to ask you something. And if you feel like I'm being too nosey, you can tell me to take a flying leap off a bridge. Okay?"

Kenzie nervously giggled . . . and not over the corny colloquialism. "Sure. Shoot."

Shirley leaned in, gestured to the faded bruises on Kenzie's arm, and locked eyes with her. "Does he know you're here?"

Kenzie crossed her arms and withdrew from the table. She really hoped a lecture wasn't coming. "No."

"You didn't tell him where you were going?"

Kenzie shook her head.

"Will he be able to figure it out? Does he know about this place?"

Christ, lady, Kenzie thought, *would you drop it?* But she answered, "I mentioned it in passing about a year ago. Something about my mom's father, whom I never met, ran some bed and breakfast down south. Didn't even say Texas." A lie. She mentioned the town of Penumbra in South Texas, but Paul probably wasn't even listening when she said it. There was no way he'd remember such a detail.

"Have you told *anyone* else about this visit? Maybe a friend, someone who might tell him where you went?"

"No. No one knows." A hint of annoyance crept into Kenzie's voice.

Shirley caught it and quickly backed off. "Okay then," she said, smiling, "I want you and the children to stay here. For as long as needed. Or as long as you like."

Thank GOD! Kenzie almost screamed. Instead, she sighed sharply in relief.

"And I promise, no more questions. We just need to know if there might be any trouble heading our way. We want things to remain quiet and peaceful here. I have that responsibility to my guests."

"Thank you. Thank you *so* much." But Kenzie's relief was short lived. She thought of the few dollars left in her wallet and didn't know if Shirley planned to charge her for the stay. She assumed she wouldn't but needed to address the issue to be sure. "Um . . ." Her cheeks grew red. "I . . . I have very little money left and I—"

"You're our guest. We're family. And that's what family does. We don't expect you to pay a dime."

"Oh, no. I couldn't." The words slipped out, an involuntary response based on politeness and pride. *What're you saying, stupid? Shut up! SHUT UP!* "I mean, I-I-I could get a job. Maybe in town. To at least pay *something.*"

"Nonsense. Your job will be here. Helping me run the inn."

"Really?" Kenzie could go for that. Rather than feeling like a charity case, she could earn her keep.

"Yes. We'd love to have some young bodies around here for a change. It'll help liven up the place."

Kenzie couldn't help but notice all the *we* pronouns. The place appeared deserted. Maybe after being married for so long it became second nature. A hard habit to break. Or maybe, "Is there someone else that works here with you?"

"No. Just me."

Kenzie motioned to the front of the house. "I didn't see any cars outside. Are you currently closed? Is this the off season?"

"No. We're always open. But business isn't what it used to be. Except for the occasional lost soul wandering in, there's only the two women upstairs in Three-A and B who have been here for quite some time. Actually, close to three decades now."

"Wow. That's great. They've been coming here that long?"

"No. They've *been* here that long. Showed up one evening and loved the place so much, they never left. I couldn't be happier with the arrangement since it's steady cash flow. I mean, Jack, God rest his soul, wasn't current with his life insurance so after the . . . incident . . . happened, I could've really been bad off. Having their steady rent, along with the money I'd accumulated over my travels, not only kept the lights on and bills paid, but kept me in the black. Plus, I'm a thrifty old bird. I won't bore you with the details, but let's say I've invested wisely in things guaranteeing a prosperous future."

Kenzie wished she could say the same. But today's visit was a good start for both her and the kids alike.

~

"Go on," Lilly egged Tim on.

With their backs to the house, the kids stood a couple yards from the woodpile. Thankfully, the grass around it had been trimmed enough to avoid stepping on any snakes that might be lurking about.

Lilly playfully pushed Tim's shoulder, nudging him to check out the pile. Instead of moving ahead, Tim slid sideways, out of reach. Lilly clucked like a chicken over his reaction.

"Nuh-uh," Tim said. "Am not!"

"C'mon. I'll show you there's nothing to be scared of."

The girl went for a closer look. The once neatly stacked pile was now in disarray, some spots appearing more like the preparation for a bonfire. Lilly moved to the backside, carefully watching where she stepped, kicking rotten pieces of wood out of her way. Rounding the corner, her eyes widened.

Tim noticed the expression. "What? What is it?"

Lilly didn't answer, only bent over, leaned in. "Come here. Look at this."

"Wha?" Tim crept forward, his eyes shifting between the wood pile and his sister's face, hoping for a clue that might lessen the shock of what he was about to see. But his sister remained silent.

A rear section of the pile was hollowed out, forming a shallow cove roomy enough to house a large dog. The ground inside was a nest of leaves and twigs, and the whole thing reeked with a musky odor.

When Tim stepped in front of Lilly to inspect their find, she took full advantage of the moment, lunging forward and poking his ribs from behind. "Boo!"

He yelped, shot straight up, and landed off balance. Before he fell and hurt himself, Lilly caught him by the collar and eased him to the ground.

"I'm tellin' Ma!" he said.

She pulled him back up to his feet and straightened his rumpled shirt. "I was just playing with you. Chill out."

"'S'not funny." He pouted, not liking the fact she got him good.

Lilly threw her arm around his shoulder and squeezed tight. "Said I was only playing. I won't do it anymore, okay? C'mon. Let's go back inside."

She guided him to the house. As they crossed the yard, Lilly suddenly shivered over the odd sensation they were being watched. Her eyes instantly zeroed in on the third floor.

A curtain at one of the windows was partially pulled back.

She abruptly halted and Tim glanced up at her, confused. Seeing the uneasy look on her face, he asked what the problem was.

Back at the window, the curtain dropped and went still.

"Someone's watching us." She pointed at the far window on the third floor.

Tim looked, saw no one, and eyed her suspiciously before pulling free and continuing on. "Told you it's not funny," he said, trudging up the porch steps.

But Lilly was not smiling while the house's cold, dark shadow loomed over her.

~

While the children stuffed their faces with warm apple pie and vanilla ice cream, Kenzie and Shirley settled for another cup of coffee.

Elbows propped on the table, Shirley held the cup to her lower lip and watched the kids in both admiration and fascination.

In between bites, Lilly asked, "Who's upstairs?"

Shirley feigned surprise. "And how do you know someone's up

there?"

"'Cause I see them at the window. Well, I can't really *see* who they are because they're peeking out. But they keep watching me. It's kinda weird."

"You shouldn't be bothered by it," Shirley said. "They're probably admiring what a beautiful young lady you are. I promise, they're very nice people."

"These are the two women you were telling me about earlier?" Kenzie said.

Shirley nodded and her face lit up. "Myrna and Lucille." She addressed Lilly, "Myrna is the one you've been seeing. She's a sweet woman. A little shy, that's all. Nothing to worry about." She turned back to Kenzie. "Some might consider her antisocial and a bit . . . abrasive. But she's just set in her ways. She's Lucille's nurse."

"Oh," Kenzie said. "Lucille's sick?"

"Yes and no. She's very old. And I'm afraid her light is fading fast."

"Wha?" Tim said.

Shirley leaned closer to the boy. "She's dying, son."

"Ooah," Tim said and returned to his pie and ice cream, which he found much more interesting anyway.

"If she's that bad, wouldn't it be better for her to be in a hospice or something? Instead of all the way out here. Wouldn't they offer better care?"

"Well, she doesn't want to—" Shirley paused and faked a smile for the children, who were listening to a much too adult conversation.

Kenzie picked up on it also. "Hey, guys. Why don't you take your dessert into the living room and check out what's on TV?"

They didn't have to be told twice. They were practically out of the room before she finished the sentence, clopping like Clydesdales through the open doorway. Their heavy steps rattled the china in the cabinet. She reminded herself to, once again, have that discussion sooner rather than later about treading much lighter around the place.

With the kids now out of earshot, Kenzie turned to Shirley. "Okay. I'm sorry. You were saying?"

Shirley checked the doorway behind her, the one leading to the lobby, then said, barely above a whisper, "The poor woman wants to pass here. In her own home." She nodded and looked around. "Yes, this is her home now and has been for nearly thirty years. And Myrna is all the care she's requested. Medically speaking, I suppose they have everything they need up there. I'm assuming that, of course. I haven't been in either room since handing them the keys."

"*Seriously*? You haven't been in their rooms in that long? For almost thirty years? C'mon."

Shirley shrugged. "I respect their privacy. They've been model guests."

"But what about housekeeping? General upkeep?"

"Myrna does all that. She's quite the multitasker. I simply provide her with fresh linens, cleaning supplies, stuff like that. I'm not saying I like her doing my job, but I do respect her level of dedication."

Kenzie still found it hard to believe Shirley hadn't been in either room for nearly three decades. Wasn't she curious if they'd broke something or messed her stuff up? Then again, it was two old ladies up there, not a pair of teenagers. She decided against pressing the matter any further. "So . . . does Lucille ever come out?"

"No. She's an invalid. Can't walk. Can't really be moved. And her health has been rapidly declining the past few months. The poor soul lies in bed and patiently waits for her day to come. Myrna has been caring for her, trying to make her remaining time as pleasant as possible."

Kenzie's breathing grew shallow. Although it had been years since she lost her mother, the wounds never healed. What Shirley was saying sounded way too familiar. And at the risk of coming off as selfish and superficial, she hoped to never meet Lucille or be forced to inhale that sickening scent of the dying.

Wiping her sweaty palms on her pants, Kenzie faked a smile and hoped Shirley hadn't noticed she'd temporarily drifted from their conversation. "What about Myrna? Will she be down anytime soon?"

"Well, as I mentioned before, she's a little shy at first. But she'll come around. It's like leaving out a bowl of milk for a stray cat. You don't try to bring the cat over to the bowl. You leave it alone, and it'll eventually come by its own accord. That's the best way to describe Myrna. When the time is right, she'll come to you."

NINE

"*THIS? THIS* **IS WHAT YOU** took from my desk?" Lilly said, kneeling on the Jeep's tailgate. She held up a twice-read, dog-eared copy of a Harry Potter book, a thesaurus, and a pocket-sized dictionary. "Maaaa!"

Kenzie shrugged and continued digging through trash bags to find Tim's underwear for tomorrow. "Sorry, babe. We'll see about getting you something new to read when we go into town. Deal?"

Lilly loudly huffed and continued her search for more books.

It was after lunch. Kenzie and the kids weeded through their belongings in the back of the SUV, gathering what they needed for the upcoming stay. She didn't want to seem presumptuous and bring all the boxes and trash bags into the house. So, for now, they cherry picked the essentials. Unfortunately, since the packing was done so haphazardly, it was taking much longer than expected.

The mess was a palpable reminder of the fear Kenzie felt only three days earlier, which, now in the safety and seclusion of their new "home," felt like a lifetime ago. Still, she couldn't fool herself into any false sense of security. Paul wasn't one to forgive and forget if ever slighted, cheated, or, God forbid, betrayed. Depending on the severity of the offense, he was prone to let things fester until finally exploding into action (usually with alcohol as his accelerant). Stealing his fanny pack (she almost snickered at how ridiculous it sounded) containing the few hundred dollars pretty much guaranteed there'd be a price to pay if he ever caught up with them.

Doubt suddenly clamped over her brain. What type of mother would put her children in such a situation, especially if the man planned to seek them out for retribution? But Kenzie only had to remind herself of the way Paul leered at her nearly naked daughter and any doubt quickly evaporated. Instead, the better question was what type of mother would she be if she chose to ignore it and they stayed?

She had done the right thing. But that didn't get rid of the need to constantly check over her shoulder. She stared down the long driveway overtaken by dense woods. The house's isolation was both blessing and curse. It would be hard for Paul to find, but also meant if trouble arose, it would take longer for help to arrive.

Although her cell phone had yet to get a signal since exiting the highway, Kenzie still randomly checked it, half expecting to find missed call notifications from Paul. It was silly because she bought the pay-as-you-go phone with cash in order to cover her tracks, making it impossible for him to get her new number.

It's fine, she told herself. *You're fine. We're fine. So, for once, just relax.*

She returned to rooting around through their belongings in the back of the SUV, failing to notice that someone in the third story window had been watching them the entire time.

~

During the afternoon, they settled into their new rooms on the second floor. The kids shared one with twin beds, and Kenzie claimed hers across the hall from theirs. Two smaller rooms were at the opposite end of the hallway, where the main set of stairs led down to the lobby. A second staircase leading up to the third floor sat outside their doors. Kenzie wasn't thrilled about its proximity, but out of the four rooms on the floor, hers had a private bathroom they could all share (keeping the one in the hall pristine for future guests).

While testing the comfort of her bed, Kenzie lay back, stared at the ceiling, and tried to imagine exactly where Lucille's room was in relation to hers. As callous as it was, she found it unsettling (and downright creepy) to know there was a woman slowly dying up there.

She closed her eyes to imagine Lucille's room which led her mind to travel far, far deeper than she intended it to go.

A bed, probably one with guard rails. Fresh sheets concealing a mattress stained with sweat, urine, and feces (accidents happen). Even if the dying woman was wearing a diaper or had a catheter or colostomy bag, sometimes they leak when a tube comes loose or when being changed or emptied. Yes indeed, accidents do happen. Which means the air in the room must be thick with the smell of cheap disinfectant—a flowery kind, barely masking the wretched odor of something rotting from the inside out. Being in the room for more than a few minutes leaves those god-awful smells seared in your throat, nostrils, and the very clothes you're wearing long after you've left. It stains the flesh on your hands and you can't get rid of it, no matter how often you scrub them (or use the sanitizer from the wall-mounted dispenser in the hospital hallway leading to the elevator). When you climb onto the bus to go home, you know everyone smells the decay on you (as if you've just stepped in dogshit) as you walk past them, down the aisle toward the nearest empty seat. They might give you a fleeting glance and grimace but thankfully nothing more is said. On the ride home, you slide open the window and feel grateful for the extreme wind rushing in while the bus travels at its top speed. You're blasted by air so strong it rocks you in your seat and flaps your clothes against your body, but, more importantly, flushes out your lungs. For, at that very moment, you can't smell it anymore. And all is normal. Mom is healthy and safe. You're not having to watch her twitch and groan in her sleep. Or feed her that pureed food. (What in the world is that pink sludge on the plate—oh, of course! Pureed ham. Mmmm-mmm. "C'mon, Ma. It's good for you. Please eat it.") You feed her spoonful after spoonful as she stares blankly ahead, a zombie doped up on engineered poison trying to destroy the natural poison spreading and gaining the higher ground in the battle raging within her body. As she chews and swallows the sludge, the cords in her neck pull taut beneath her flesh. You never noticed that vein before. Was it always there? Or is it because she's lost even more weight and her skin is stretched even tighter across her skeletal frame. You scoop another spoonful, realizing it might be too much for her to handle. She could spit it up on you. Or worse . . . choke. You pause, eye the spoonful, and glance at the open doorway to see if anyone is out in the hall. Spotting no one, you listen. The hospital sounds deserted. No one would be around to help if she chokes. You're not trained to react and even if you did, you could do more damage to her already frail body, right? No one would blame you if you didn't act. You could say you panicked. They'll completely understand. Realizing it could be the answer to finally end this nightmare, you scoop a little more onto the spoon. It's now a heaping portion, one you know is too much for the dying woman to handle. You pause. In front of you sits a version of your mother looking more like someone stuck an industrial strength vacuum up her ass, flipped it on, and sucked out all that healthy meat, muscle, and happiness, until all that remains is a suit of flesh stretched so tight you can make out the shape and size of every bone in her body. So you check the hall again for any possible witnesses . . . then lift the heaping spoon. Now she's staring at you, locking eyes with you. You freeze with guilt. Her eyes leave yours, shift to the heaping mass on the spoon, then return to you. Before you can play stupid and remove most of the portion, she slowly nods once and opens her mouth, waiting for the feast she knows she can't devour. Knowing it's what she wants and before you lose your nerve, you guide the spoon into her mouth until her cracked lips press together and her teeth bite metal. You slide the spoon out, now scraped clean like an artichoke petal. And wait. She stares at you one last time and attempts a genuine yet pathetic smile, one you'll never forget. You slide your chair slightly back to give her room. Then, without chewing, she swallows hard, her throat flexing, straining to take the load. You push back a little farther and she gags, starts convulsing, and fighting for air. She falls back on the bed. Thrashes wildly. Claws at the sheets. You watch. First, her. Then the door. Then her again. You watch as she—

Kenzie's eyes snapped open.

Stop it!

She slowly sat up on the bed, planted both feet on the floor, and wiped the sweat from her hairline.

The sweet sound of children's laughter floated in from across the hall.

She took a deep, soothing breath to bring her back to the present, where a new chapter of life had begun. A do-over she was extremely fortunate to have.

Kenzie sat silently and absorbed the sound of their joy.

The kids seemed truly happy there. Back at home, they were forced to bunk together since a two-bedroom apartment was all she and Paul could afford. But earlier, Shirley offered them separate rooms. Lilly and Tim exchanged a glance and, with little hesitation, declined, choosing instead to remain together. Although Kenzie would've loved for them to have their own rooms for the first time, it made her happy they were acting as a team, looking out for each other in this new environment. It also meant one less room they'd be occupying that could be rented and, in turn, make their stay less intrusive.

Kenzie moved to the doorway and glanced into the hall to take in their new living situation. Her eyes stopped on the shadowy staircase next to the kids' room, the one leading to the third floor.

Shirley informed her the top level contained only two bedrooms, a hallway linen closet, and the entrance to the attic. Except for restocking clean sheets or towels or fetching something from attic storage, the third floor was to remain void of traffic in the interest of maintaining tenant privacy.

Yet Kenzie found herself at the bottom of the stairs, looking up. Shirley promised her a complete tour of the house once her "training" began tomorrow, but, for now, Kenzie fancied a little preview.

She glanced up the carpeted steps leading to the small landing that wrapped around and continued to the next floor. Given her low angle, peering through the balusters on the second flight offered no further insight, so she started climbing.

The stairs creaked under her tiny frame, each one groaning louder as if the house objected to the intrusion. She winced at the noise and debated whether to turn back, but her legs kept moving.

Finally reaching the middle landing, she stared up at the third floor. It was shadowy and still. From her limited vantage point, she saw two hall windows on the right, their curtains drawn and fabric much thicker than the sheer ones used on the lower levels.

Kenzie ascended a few more steps.

To her left was an open entryway, then two doors, and a final one facing her at the end of the hall. The middle pair must have been the bedrooms, while the fourth at the end, the linen closet. Kenzie eyed the open doorway and caught the edge of a step, confirming it was the attic entrance . . . and making it an ideal place to start snooping.

Her damp palm peeled off the polished bannister. She stepped up onto the third floor, padded across the carpet runner, and ducked into the cove at the base of the attic stairs.

Inside, only the first half dozen wooden steps were visible. Beyond that, darkness swallowed what remained. Either the attic had no windows or, more likely, there was a closed door used for additional insulation at the top of the landing.

While feeling for a light switch along the wall, the wood creaked from somewhere within the blackness above.

Her spine stiffened.

Kenzie slowly looked up. Assuming there was a door up there, the noise must have come from behind it. Probably the nurse, Myrna, retrieving something from storage and making her way back down. Kenzie debated whether to run before being spotted (since she wasn't supposed to be up there in the first place) or stay and introduce herself.

Then the darkness stirred above.

Her eyes narrowed and caught movement.

Wait.

Was someone standing up there? At the top of the stairs?

Another creak descended out of the void. Louder, which also meant . . .

Closer.

This time, she swore it came from within the stairwell. In fact, only a few steps above her.

Okay, screw this! Kenzie quickly turned, exited the attic cove, and strode back down the hall. Taking two steps at a time to reach the floor below, she refused to slow down long enough to check over her shoulder, terrified a hand might jut out from between the balusters, grab her by the hair, and drag her back upstairs into the pitch-black attic.

Once reaching the safety of the second floor, she paused outside the kids' room to regain her composure.

Geez, you've got some imagination.

She exhaled and straightened her rumpled shirt. *Okay-okay-okay. Time to start actin' like an adult again.*

The kids screamed when Kenzie jumped into the room—wide-eyed, teeth baring, and with splayed fingers hooked like claws. "Bwah-hah-hah-hah-hah!" she howled at them.

Caught off guard, Tim was on the floor immersed in his comic book while Lilly was on the bed cradling *Harry Potter and the Prisoner of Azkaban*. The girl jolted and dropped the book. Although Tim giggled after realizing it was only Mom messing around, his sister wasn't so amused. Before Lilly could complain, Kenzie rushed them, tossed Tim onto her bed, and smothered both with kisses.

As the family continued laughing and goofing around, their commotion concealed the creak of a floorboard out in the hall, around the corner and at the foot of the stairs.

TEN

NIGHT CREPT OVER THE HOUSE. Most of its occupants retired to the living room, relaxing after a delicious meal of oven-roasted chicken, mashed potatoes, fresh green beans, and the leftover mac and cheese from lunch.

Kenzie, Lilly, and Tim helped Shirley prepare dinner, another feast when compared to their usual meals comprised of items served out of a box, from a can, or previously frozen like a popsicle. Kenzie was beyond grateful to have such delicious food but if she and the kids kept eating like this, they'd have to expand their wardrobe—not in selection, but size. Such meals probably weren't the norm, just Shirley showing hospitality to her new guests. In any case, Kenzie felt like she'd balloon up by week's end unless getting a little exercise, even if it meant taking the kids for a brisk walk through the woods to do some exploring.

While assisting Shirley with the food, Kenzie received a few more tidbits of info about the third-floor occupants. The subject was inadvertently brought up when she, Kenzie, told Lilly and Tim to set the table for five, the fifth spot being for Myrna. Shirley quickly corrected her and said to only set four spots, since the women dined (much later) in their own rooms. Because of this, two additional food plates were always made, covered with cellophane, placed on a tray, and left

44

outside 3A (Myrna's room).

For now, Shirley would take care of it until Kenzie was trained on the various protocols. Kenzie recalled her third floor heebie-jeebie incident earlier and felt grateful to be temporarily spared the task.

"Is Myrna really that shy that she only eats in her room?" Kenzie asked.

"Well, not so much shy than just being particular of who she dines with. She prefers to eat with Lucille. After spending so much time together, they act like an old married couple. They're quite the late-night eaters too. Usually not sitting down for supper until well after I've gone to bed."

"So, when do you bring the food up? Before going to sleep?"

"No. Usually after I've eaten and done the dishes. Myrna has her own refrigerator up there for storing Lucille's medications. She keeps the plates chilled until they're both ready to eat. Then heats them up in her microwave."

"Sounds like she has her own little apartment up there."

Shirley shrugged. "Those rooms do have their own bathroom and a small kitchen. It was part of the additional renovations we made throughout the house after Jack died. With such amenities, you can understand why you won't see much of Myrna. There's really no reason for her to come down except to get fresh air and avoid cabin fever. Or to be social, which probably isn't going to happen."

"And Lucille? She never comes down?"

"Nope. Bedridden. Remember?"

Kenzie remembered. She simply wanted reassurance.

~

While Tim and Lilly helped their mother wash and dry the dishes, Shirley disappeared with two plates on a tray. Upon returning, she found Kenzie and the children hunkered down in the living room, Lilly with her Harry Potter book and Tim watching an old Boris Karloff movie on television.

Shirley plopped on the couch holding a pair of tennis shoes.

Kenzie acknowledged the sneakers. "Going for a walk?" If the woman said yes, Kenzie was game to join her.

Shirley struggled to slip on her shoe. "Me? Heavens no. I don't go out after dark. It's time to do a little laundry." She kicked up a foot to show off her Nikes, so white and pristine they looked brand new. "When you have feet as flat as mine and been on them all day, these make standing on that hard linoleum much more tolerable."

Kenzie slid to the edge of her chair. "Well, I'll help you."

"I know you will. But not tonight. Tonight, you relax. You've had a long day." Shirley noticed the movie playing on the television was *The Old Dark House*. "Ahhhh, Boris Karloff. He was my favorite as a little girl. Had the biggest crush on him."

Lilly glanced up from her book and gave Shirley a soured look, as if someone had waved dogshit under the girl's nose.

Shirley waited for a nice close-up of Karloff to appear onscreen. "Tim, do you know that's Frankenstein?"

The boy stared at the actor's visage in the film—bearded, scarred, and droopy-eyed. "Nuh-uh. Frankenstein has a square head and bolts on his neck."

"She means it's the same actor," Kenzie added.

Tim studied Karloff in the role of the brutish, alcoholic butler. "No way. This guy has a round head."

Lilly lowered her book. "It's all make-up, ya dork. It's the same guy."

Tim looked as if they were all suddenly speaking Pig Latin. "Whuh?" He turned back to the television and ignored them.

The three ladies shared a smile, then Shirley stood, groaning in the process.

"I really wish you'd let me give you a hand," Kenzie said.

"Don't worry, there'll be plenty of that starting tomorrow. But tonight, you're still my guest. So relax and cherish your time with the little ones."

Before Kenzie could further object, Shirley left the room.

On television, the howling wind and rain pounded the old mansion while Karloff crept around its dark corridors by candlelight. Kenzie noticed Tim gripping the pillow tight as the suspenseful music swelled. The boy was scared.

"Tim, why don't you put on something else? Something funny for me and your sister."

He turned to her. "But I'm watching this, Ma."

"It's not too scary?"

Tim thought about it for a moment. "This? Nah. It's like . . . in black and white and stuff."

She raised an eyebrow. "Then it's not gonna give you scary dreams tonight?"

"No way." He went back to the movie.

Lilly and Kenzie exchanged a look that read, "Yep. He'll be

46

scared." Then Lilly returned to her book.

Feeling a little anxious herself, Kenzie pulled out her cell and checked for a signal. Still nothing. Eventually it would get one and she dreaded its screen would be filled with missed call notifications and threatening texts from Paul.

Would you chill? He doesn't even have this number!

Still, it would take her a long time before she could push him to the back of her mind like that.

ELEVEN

WITH THE SHEET PULLED UP to the bridge of his nose, Tim was scared.

He now wished he'd listened to his mom earlier about changing the channel on that horror movie. Unlike Lilly, it had taken him a good hour to relax once the lights went out. Furthering his uneasiness, he wasn't used to the new room. The closet (its door, of course, closed) was beside him, unlike at home where it was at the foot of his bed—conveniently out of sight, out of mind. In his new setting, he faced the door and refused to put his back to it. His sister's bed, usually to his right was now at his left. At home, their beds were pushed against opposite walls to make a play area on the floor between them. But here, although still parallel, they were positioned in the middle of the room. Without a wall to nestle his back against, any sense of security vanished. It was now imperative to remain in the middle of the mattress to avoid getting yanked under the bed from either side.

When his mom tucked them in for the night and retired to her own room, he figured he'd doze off rather quickly after such an eventful day. The news reported a storm rolling in, and he hoped to be sound asleep before it hit since thunder and lightning made him nervous. At least (once again) he'd ride things out with Lilly by his side. But as the minutes ticked by, all the calming comforts he normally relied on began to crumble away.

First, when Lilly was still awake, they lay in bed and talked about Shirley being nice and how big the house was. As the conversation dwindled and the silence stretched between them, Tim asked, "What do you think Paul's doing right now?" There was no reply for a few seconds, then a light snore came from Lilly's bed. Knowing she was a heavy sleeper, he might as well have been alone in the room now.

His covers inched a little higher.

Then the hall light glowing under their closed bedroom door shut off. Mom was officially going to bed. Even as minimal as the light had been, without it, the room was now plunged into nearly complete darkness.

The covers rose even more.

He stared out until his eyes adjusted enough to see the closet door was still closed.

Tim remained vigilant a little while longer until his lids eventually drooped and sealed shut.

~

It wasn't the rumble of thunder that pulled Tim awake but the heavy breathing over his shoulder.

He first thought Lilly was sleeping with her mouth open again. But the more he shrugged off slumber, Tim realized it wasn't the same sound he'd grown accustomed to after sharing a room with her for so long. No, what was coming from that side of the room sounded more like Jell-O extruding through a rubber tube.

There was a moist wheeze.

Sickly. Monstrous.

Then awful sucking and smacking sounds, like a teenage couple awkwardly kissing.

Lightning strobed the room and, to Tim's horror, he noticed the closet door was ajar. His heart raced. He lay frozen, bound by dread, too afraid to roll over and see what crawled out of the closet and what it was doing to his sister.

Please, let this be a scary dream, he thought. *Just a scary dream.*

The sucking ceased. Then the heavy wheezing slowed to a stop. In such silence, the seconds ticked by like minutes.

Tim had to see if the thing was gone. And, more importantly, if Lilly was okay. With his lower lip trembling, he rotated only his upper body to avoid making the bedsprings squeak.

Framed against the lightning-strobed window, a skeletal-like figure stooped on the opposite side of Lilly's bed, hovering inches from her face. The young girl must have still been asleep, or the room's silence would've been shredded by her blood curdling screams.

As his eyes slowly adjusted, Tim could see it wasn't some monster standing over his sister, but an old woman. Her disheveled gray hair hung low, concealing not only her face, but half of Lilly's as well. The wet smacking sound resumed.

Tim swallowed hard, causing his dry throat to loudly click.

In response, the woman's head snapped up in his direction.

Tim gasped.

Then a floorboard squeaked in the murky corner.

The boy's eyes flicked over and saw a second person in the room with them, a voyeur crouching in the blackness beside the overstuffed chair. Once spotted, the figure grunted and ducked behind the piece of furniture.

Tim's heart beat triple-time. Outside the window, another bolt of lightning blasted the sky. The room strobed again to reveal the old woman at Lilly's bedside was completely naked. Her body was wrinkled and bumpy, the skin bulging in areas as if something were forcing its way through. Sagging, shriveled breasts hung to her doughy stomach. Her overgrown pubic region spread across her lap like a nest of daddy long leg spiders. The long, disheveled locks kept her face concealed. Ribbons of drool stretched out from under the matted mess . . . and down to the parted lips of Lilly's open mouth.

Her full attention now on Tim, the woman groaned and reached out for him, taking a step around Lilly's bed, moving closer to his.

Tim whimpered and slid back to the opposite side of the mattress, putting as much distance between him and the hunched, naked crone as possible.

She advanced, one bare foot slapping across the floorboard while the other dragged behind, her long toenails raking the wood like the sharp claws of an animal.

In response, Tim scooted farther away until teetering on the edge of the mattress . . . then fell straight to the floor.

Hitting the ground with a loud thud, he prayed the noise would wake his mother or Shirley downstairs and send them rushing into the room to investigate.

Tim lay petrified in fear. Another flash of lightning revealed their bedroom door was half open. He was about to flip around and make a run for it when a shadow stretched across his escape route.

His exit now blocked, Tim slid under the bed for cover. While checking to make sure he was dead center of the box spring, he saw wrinkled bare feet in the strip of space between the ground and the bottom of the bed skirt, exactly where he'd been lying only seconds earlier.

She stood over him.

Tim prayed the mattress and box spring wouldn't rip off its frame like the flimsy roof of a tin shack during a tornado, leaving him completely exposed and vulnerable. He slid away to the opposite side of the bed. Dreading she might crouch for a peek under, Tim whimpered and covered his mouth with trembling hands. He cried and squeezed his eyes shut.

His heart pounded so hard in his eardrums it drowned out all other sounds. His head spun. Body tremored. Then a deafening silence and an utter blackness cut it all off like the flipping of a switch.

When his eyes snapped back open, she was gone.

A portion of the skirt was raised at the end of the bed. Tim yanked his bare feet up and away from the opening. Although he couldn't see the woman, he felt she was there, kneeling, peering in at him.

His entire body shuddered uncontrollably as if dunked in an icy bath. He tried to scream for help, but fear continued paralyzing his vocal cords.

Terrified the woman hadn't left the room but was hiding and trying to trick him into coming out, Tim checked his surroundings with each strobe brought on by the storm. He pushed up on the bed to make sure she wasn't on top, waiting for him to slide out.

Sucking in deep breaths, Tim steeled himself to make a run for it. Not only would he have to bolt out of the room, he'd have to cross the dark hall and pray his mother's door wasn't locked. If it were, he'd be trapped out there with whomever had been in his room, now possibly roaming the hallway.

"One . . ." Tim whispered.

"Two . . ."

On three, he made his move.

TWELVE

KENZIE SNAPPED AWAKE HEARING HER son shrieking in terror and calling her name. As she flipped on the bedside lamp, Tim burst through the door.

"Maaaaa!"

"Wha? Whaat? What's the matter?"

The boy dove onto his mother's waist and held on tight. He buried his head against her belly, soiling her sleeping shirt with snot and tears. She peeled him off and stared into his terrified eyes. "Tim, what is it?"

His lower lip quivered for a few seconds then, "The scary woman! She's trying to get me!"

Staring at her son, Kenzie knew the boy was okay. Scared shitless, but *physically* all right. She glanced toward the kids' room and her gut twisted.

With Tim causing such a commotion, why wasn't Lilly by his side?

~

Barging into the room and flipping on the light, Kenzie exhaled in relief after finding her daughter peacefully asleep in bed.

Tim clung to his mother's side while scanning the room for the naked crone who might be hiding, waiting to attack.

Kenzie crouched in front of Tim. "Hey. Listen to me. You were only having a bad dream because of that scary movie. That's all."

Tim frantically shook his head. "No! She was here! She was standing over Lilly. Messing with her. It sounded like she was kissing her."

"*What?* Who is *she?*"

"The lumpy old woman. She was . . . she was naked."

"*Naked?*"

"Yes!" Tim's cheeks grew even more flushed and guilt washed over his face. "But I-I-I didn't mean to look at her. You're not mad at me, are you? I mean, I couldn't help it. She had no clothes on."

Exhaling sharply, Kenzie paused before speaking. "No. I'm not mad at you. I only thought . . ." She looked back at Lilly. The kid was a heavy sleeper, but this was ridiculous. How could she not have woken, even now with the light on and them conversing at her bedside?

"Lilly? Wake up, hon."

The girl groaned. Kenzie gave her a shake. "Lilly. Come on. Wake up."

Lilly stirred and her lids fluttered at the bright light. "Whaaaa . . .?" She wiped the sleep from her eyes, coughed, and rubbed her neck. "What's going on?" The words were croaked out. She cleared her throat and massaged it a little more.

"Did you see anybody in here tonight?"

"Huh?"

Kenzie repeated the question and received a confused look. "Ahhh, yeah. Tim."

"Besides your brother. Was there a woman in here?"

She shrugged and glanced at Tim, who looked petrified and hung on her every word. Lilly returned to her mom. "What's up with him?"

"Just answer the question. Was anyone here, besides you and Tim?"

"No. Why?" Then it suddenly became clear. Lilly sighed. "Oh, God. Was he having another one of his stupid nightmares?" She plopped down and pulled the covers over her head. As far as she was concerned, the conversation was over.

Kenzie turned to Tim. "See? It was a bad dream. Your imagination playing with you after watching that old horror movie which, by the way, are now completely off limits."

"What happened?" a woman asked.

Tim yelped and slid behind his mother.

A puffy-eyed Shirley stood in the bedroom doorway, yawning and tightening the belt on her pink terry cloth robe. "What's going on?"

~

As thunder rumbled in the distance, Kenzie sat at the kitchen table and blew on a hot cup of coffee. Shirley sat across from her. Through the open doorway of the dining room, they could see Tim lying on the living room couch, cocooned in a blanket with only his face exposed. Although exhausted, he kept close tabs on his mother, making sure she didn't leave his sight.

"Kenzie, dear, I can assure you in the near thirty years they've been here, I've never witnessed either of them sleepwalking. Besides, it couldn't have been Lucille since it's my understanding the poor soul can't walk anymore. As for Myrna, although the woman can be extremely forthright, she's far too modest to be prancing around naked at her age. Especially in front of children."

"I know. I know. I think it just might be the stress from all the sudden change," Kenzie said. "First night in a new place. Unfamiliar surroundings. The storm. That scary movie. He's had night terrors before. All that stuff could've triggered another episode. His mind got the best of him." In a way, she couldn't blame her son. She thought of her own episode yesterday, on the attic stairs. And how restless she was lying alone in bed last night, staring at the ceiling, unable to let go of the fact a woman lay dying somewhere above her.

They were all on edge. Well, maybe not Lilly, who was still sleeping like a log upstairs. Quite the opposite from her brother over there on the couch.

Kenzie checked on him again and found the boy asleep. It was about time.

She took a sip of coffee and noticed the first rays of dawn breaking outside the kitchen window. The storm had passed. "Well, I'm sorry we caused such a commotion. Guess now that the sun is up, we can forget about going back to bed, huh?"

Shirley grabbed a notebook off the counter. "Then I guess it's as good a time as any to start your training."

Excited, Kenzie wiggled in her seat and furiously rubbed her hands together. "Like Mister Miyagi and Daniel-san?"

Shirley looked confused.

"C'mon. You know . . . wax on? Wax off?" *The Karate Kid* was one of her mom's favorite movies, which meant Kenzie, herself, had seen it numerous times growing up.

The reference still eluded the woman.

"Never mind," Kenzie said. "Not important." She slid her chair closer while Shirley thumbed through the book. The pages were completely covered in writing, with more black ink than actual page white.

"Whoa," Kenzie said.

"Oh, don't worry. Most of these are recipes, old grocery lists, and other scribble-scrabbles." She flipped to the middle of the book. "Ah, here we go."

There was a neatly constructed list divided into two columns, which appeared a hell-of-a-lot more manageable to Kenzie.

Shirley skimmed her notes and closed the book. "Ya know what? How about we start simple? With an official tour of all the rooms. Well . . . most of them."

~

Their first stop was the large laundry room with its full washer and dryer, floor mounted utility tub, and built-in shelving to the ceiling. An ironing station was set up in the corner along with a rolling garment rack.

A few steps in, Shirley halted and slid back the ball of her foot three times across the linoleum floor. Then she stepped aside and pointed at the spot where the odd gesture was made.

"That's where your grandfather was found."

Kenzie did a double take at Shirley, not sure if she heard correctly. "Found?"

"Found dead, of course."

Kenzie stared at the floor and retreated a few paces. "H-here? I thought you said it was some sort of animal attack. How did it get in here?"

"It chased him through the backdoor and cornered him. Trapped him here. Apparently, it was quite cunning."

Kenzie looked over her shoulder and into the kitchen, tracing the route back to the spot. "Shirley? You mind if I ask what kind of animal it was?"

The woman shrugged. "They thought it might've been a coyote or bobcat. Maybe even a wild dog. But they never found any traces of fur. Not here or stuck to any of the pieces strewn about." Her last sentence made Kenzie's eyes widen. "So, the coroner ruled it simply 'death by animal unknown' or 'unknown animal,' or something along those lines."

"God. I'm so sorry."

Shirley silently studied the spot for a few moments. "I often feel like a small part of him is still here with us. I mean, I can't imagine the coroner and his gang got all the pieces. Betcha that's why, huh?"

Kenzie's jaw dropped.

"Oh. Please excuse the gallows humor. Sometimes it's necessary to help keep one's sanity, don't you think? In any case . . ." Shirley waved a hand around the room. "Things have to be kept spotless here, especially when cleaning all the white linens we have in the house. I make sure to dust the entire area and mop the floors once a week. Tuesday mornings to be exact."

Kenzie nodded but thought, *Because things would all go to hell if it was done Tuesday* afternoon?

"Come on. Come over here," Shirley said, motioning to the dryer. "I want to show you how to open the door on this thing. It sticks and the hinges are loose, so it has to be opened just right or it'll break off. Other than that, it works perfectly fine and I hope to milk it for another few years. C'mere, let me show you what I'm talking about."

Kenzie moved forward but made a wide berth around the spot where dear ol' Grandpa was ripped apart. Otherwise, it would've felt too much like walking over the man's grave.

~

The remaining tour was standard stuff. Kenzie was guided through the two bedrooms on the first floor, one of them being the master suite (Shirley's room), followed by the two unoccupied quarters on the second level. She was shown the location of the gas and water valves, air conditioning units and their return air grilles, the fuse box, and hot water heater. A large storage closet opposite the dining room housed cleaning supplies, a toolbox, air filters, spare fuses, along with other various odds and ends like inn stationery and postcards, candles, and spare light bulbs. Hall closets on the upper levels each contained fresh bed linens, towels, a vacuum cleaner, and a broom with dustpan.

Unbelievably, the house only had one phone: a black, push button relic sitting at the front desk.

"Wow," Kenzie said. "That thing still works?"

Shirley picked up the handpiece and checked for a dial tone. "Sure does. Except when water gets into the line from a heavy rain, which, unfortunately, can sometimes knock it out for days."

~

Climbing the steps to the third floor, Kenzie felt a drop of sweat roll out from under her arm and tickle her ribs.

Hopefully, the remaining part of the tour would avoid any introduction to the elderly tenants. Especially Lucille. Seeing the terminal woman would only bring forth a deluge of bad memories.

Thankfully, training for the third floor took less than a minute. Since Lucille might be napping, they kept their distance, only standing on the shadowy landing. Shirley pointed down the hall and whispered, "The two bedrooms are in the middle, Myrna's being the closest. Linen closet is at the far end. Entrance to the attic is yonder. Next time I need something from it, I'll take you with me and show it to you then."

Kenzie nodded and continued acting like it was her first time being up there.

"Come on, let's head back so we don't disturb them."

On their descent, Kenzie allowed Shirley to take the lead so she could steal one last glance down the dimly lit hallway. By the time they made it to the middle landing, she'd lost complete sight of the third floor and, along with it, an uneasiness pooling in the pit of her stomach.

THIRTEEN

THREE DAYS HAD PASSED, AND Kenzie found running the inn like any other job, where a strict schedule had to be met and tasks completed before calling it a day. The house was their business, a product for their clientele, so it had to remain immaculate as if listed on the market.

Kenzie stood on the front porch, about to partake in something she'd never given a second thought to: washing windows. The extreme winds from the storm the other night left the porch windows rain-spattered and less than pristine. Shirley gave her a quick lesson in how to thoroughly clean them and left her alone to master the art of the squeegee. Kenzie dipped a sponge in the bucket containing the cleaning solution, gave it a slight wring to remove excess water, then soaked and scrubbed the window on the front door until it was soapy. The sponge was exchanged for the squeegee and its first vertical swipe cleared the film, returning a portion of the glass to its mirror-like surface . . . one that reflected the silhouette of a man standing over her shoulder.

Spinning with her heart stuck in her throat, Kenzie retreated so fast she nearly stepped into the bucket of water.

It took her a moment to process it wasn't Paul. That he hadn't found them to reclaim his money and dish-out punishment for her thievery and betrayal.

Instead, it was a handsome man in his late twenties with a large canvas sailor's bag slung over his shoulder. Seeing her reaction, he backtracked down the porch steps to a safer distance and raised his hands in a gesture of surrender. "I'm so sorry. I didn't mean to scare you. I thought you heard me."

Once Kenzie found her breath, she forced a chuckle and gave a dismissive wave although, given past experiences, she found nothing amusing about a man sneaking up behind her. She only smiled to put him—a potential guest—at ease.

"Really, I'm sorry," he said.

"It's okay. It's okay."

They both stared at each other, waiting for the other to speak. Kenzie's first instinct was to ask who he was, and why the hell he snuck up like that. Before she could figure out a polite way to do so, he motioned to the house.

"I was told you rent rooms here. Unless I took a wrong turn somewhere back there."

"No. You're at the right place."

He cautiously moved forward and extended his hand. "I'm Ben."

She shook it. "Kenzie."

"Nice to meet you. This your place, Kenzie?"

"No, my ah . . . my grandma's." The word felt funny coming out. "She owns it. I work here. Well, just started working here."

"Cool."

Kenzie looked over at the empty parking lot. Then scanned the rest of the property.

"I walked," Ben answered before she asked. "From the main road at least. Before that I hitched a ride."

There was an awkward silence. Kenzie was still regaining her bearings after being scared half to death.

"Well, ah . . . c'mon in. I'll get Shirley so she can check you in."

She ushered him through the front door where Shirley was approaching from down the hall.

"I thought I heard a gentleman's voice," she said, smiling.

"Yes, ma'am. I'm looking to rent a room for a night or two."

While Shirley informed him of the rates, Kenzie stepped out of the conversation, but hovered in the background in case she was needed.

After Ben agreed to the price, Shirley said, "Then this way, young man, and we'll get you all taken care of." She motioned to the check-in counter then turned and addressed Kenzie. "Come, dear. You check him in."

Kenzie hesitated. "We never went over how to—"

"Because there wasn't a guest to go over it with. Now, come on, I'm sure that . . ." Shirley paused and prompted Ben for his name.

Before he could speak, Kenzie said, "Ben. His name's Ben."

He smiled at her for remembering.

"Well, I'm sure Ben wouldn't mind helping out in a brief training exercise."

"Not at all," he said, playing along good-natured.

"See? Now, get over here and let me show you what to do."

Kenzie slid up to the counter next to Shirley and opposite Ben, who kept the bulky canvas bag slung across his back. With the old woman over her shoulder walking her through the process, Kenzie had Ben fill out and sign the ledger. It was the way they'd always registered guests with no need to deviate from such a tried-and-true method.

When Kenzie retrieved the ledger from Ben, she caught him eyeing the faded bruise on her arm and quickly turned her body to hide the mark. Shirley noticed the exchange and tried to move things along, showing Kenzie where they kept the credit card imprint machine (again, old school) and its carbons.

Ben informed them he'd be staying for two nights and was given the total due. He reached in his pocket and, while keeping his bankroll below the counter and out of sight, snapped out the exact amount in cash and handed it to Kenzie. Their eyes locked briefly, and he gave her a playful smile. Kenzie blushed and looked away.

Again, Shirley took note of the interaction.

While Kenzie punched the keypad on the small safe below the counter, Shirley felt it was best to draw Ben's attention away from where the money was kept.

"So, Ben," she said, "how did you hear about our little establishment? After all, we *are* quite hidden and off the beaten path."

"A trucker I hitched a ride with recommended it. Said it was a nice, quiet place to stay. Which is exactly what I'm lookin' for."

"A trucker, huh? Would his name happen to be James?"

"Yes, ma'am. He's the one. In fact, he sends his regards."

Shirley smiled warmly and shook her head. "Such a good Christian man."

Kenzie popped up from behind the counter and waited for her next cue.

"How 'bout we give this gentleman a room on the first floor. Room One-B has fresh linens, correct?"

Kenzie nodded and fished in her pocket for the master keyring, then unlocked the wall mounted box and found his room key. "Here ya go."

"Third door down on the right," Shirley said.

Ben looked in its direction.

"We'll have sandwiches for lunch," Shirley added. "Served at noon in the dining room."

"Oh, I had a late breakfast. But thank you. What I'm really dying for is a hot shower and long nap."

Shirley nodded. "Then we'll be sure not to disturb you. And dinner will be at six. If we don't see you then, we'll make a plate and keep it in the fridge."

"Sounds great. Thank you, ma'am."

Back to Kenzie, he flashed her a warm smile and held his eye contact a few seconds longer than the norm. "And thank you, Kenzie." Then he turned and headed to his room.

Both women watched his casual stroll down the hall, moving at a snail's pace to check out what was through each open door. Having walked in his shoes only a few days earlier, Kenzie figured he was simply taking in his new environment.

But Shirley had other thoughts regarding the young man's curiosity, namely suspicion.

FOURTEEN

WITH THE NEW TENANT RESTING in 1B, the kids were told to keep their conversation to a whisper, and not stomp around while doing their after-lunch chores, distributing fresh linens to the hallway closets. They worked as a team, with Lilly carrying the pressed sheets and Tim a stack of fluffy towels.

After stealthily moving past Ben's room and restocking the closet at the end of the hall, they ascended to the second floor.

"It's just us stayin' up here," Tim said, motioning ahead. "Why do we have to switch these out already? Back home, Mom only makes us change our sheets on Sunday."

"Well, we're not at home anymore, now are we?"

Silence, except for the floorboards creaking up at them.

"Hey, Lilly? So *where* is home?"

"I don't know. I guess here. For now. Until Mom makes us leave to go somewhere else. It sucks, but we've done it before."

"But what about Paul?" Tim asked.

"What about him?"

"He wasn't around those other times."

"And?"

"And isn't he gonna be mad about all this? About us runnin' away?"

"Who cares? He's a jerk."

"I care."

"Why?"

Tim paused and stared at his feet. "'Cause he scares me. And he hurts Mom. And if he finds us . . ." The boy slowly shook his head instead of finishing his thought.

Lilly stopped. "Hey. Listen to me. Paul's gone. Mom says we don't ever have to see him again. So don't be scared of him anymore. 'Kay?"

"'Kay." Tim checked if they were still alone and leaned closer. "This place scares me too. 'Specially that naked ol' lumpy lady who came in our room."

"Oh, come on, there was no lady. You just had a nightmare from that scary movie. You even said so yourself."

"I only said that for Ma."

"Whatever. You freaked yourself out again. Admit it. Like the time you watched *War of the Worlds* and thought aliens were invading because there was a thunderstorm that night. Or the time you snuck into the living room when Paul was watching *Texas Chain Saw Massacre*. You heard a chainsaw every time a motorcycle drove by on the street and thought what's-his-face was coming to get you. Remember how bad you freaked out?"

"Yeah. Mom wasn't happy."

"Exactly. And she's not too happy about the other night either. We're trying to make a good impression here and you're all '*blah-blah-blah*, the naked old lady! The naked old lumpy lady!'"

"But what if I wasn't dreamin'? What if a lady from upstairs *did* come down to mess with us?"

"I think I'd know if someone was kissing on me like you thought you saw. I'm telling you, it was only another one of your stupid nightmares."

"I don't know."

"Okay, have you seen the naked old lumpy lady since then?"

"No. But only because Mom lets me sleep with the closet light on now."

"So . . . what? I guess if naked old ladies were like cockroaches, then closet lights would be their bug spray, huh?"

Tim thought about it for a moment. "Oooh, what if naked ol' lady had her head on a giant cockroach body? How scary would that be?!"

Lilly scoffed. "Well, she wouldn't be naked anymore, now would she?" She motioned to the linens. "C'mon. Let's quit being stupid and go put these up."

After restocking the closet, they made their way to the next level. At the third-floor landing, the kids silently peered down the long, dimly lit hallway. It was dark and claustrophobic, completely alien when compared to the warmth and coziness of the levels below. Originally told to stay off the floor out of respect for tenant privacy, they were granted permission only if they remained dead quiet.

Of course, the linen closet had to be at the far end of the hall, where they'd be forced to not only pass the attic entrance but also the two rooms housing the mysterious old women. Lilly noticed her brother's reluctance. Oddly enough, she was dreading it, too.

Her clammy palms were wrinkling the linens her mother spent all morning ironing. "Come on. Let's get this over with. Be quiet, okay?"

She stepped forward and Tim followed. In their current formation, he was on the inside track, next to all the doors.

"Wait," Lilly said. "Switch places."

"Why?"

"Look where you're standing. Do you really wanna be next to all of those?" She nodded at the doors.

Without having to be told twice, he slid around his sister and used her body as a shield. Then they started down the hall again.

Thankfully, the carpet runner was thick, cushioning their steps across the hardwood floor. Passing the open doorway to the attic, both kids peered inside at the ascending stairs. Only the first half dozen or so were visible, the rest fading to black. They continued on, keeping their eyes peeled for any shadows moving along the thin strips of light emanating from under the bedroom doors.

The kids moved silently, making their way to the closet. Lilly twisted its white porcelain knob and the door creaked open. She quickly added her folded sheets to the small stack on the middle shelf, took the towels from Tim, and put them in their proper place. Then the kids turned and looped back for the stairs.

Tim, apparently feeling more confident, stood between his sister and the doors this time.

"Hey," Lilly whispered. "You're not scared?"

"No. Course not."

She waited for him to take the lead. Once they passed Lucille's bedroom, Lilly shoved her brother at Myrna's door.

Before Tim slammed into it, she grabbed him and safely reeled him back. But the boy already let off a loud gasp and squeal, heavily stomping away from the door.

It was a harmless scare she couldn't pass up. Snickering, she pulled him closer and hugged him tight.

Tim looked up at her with a mixture of betrayal and anger burning in his eyes.

Although she knew he was upset, Lilly still giggled and whispered, "Thought you weren't scared? Boy, you should've seen the look on your f—"

A floorboard creaked.

They exchanged a look, knowing neither had moved to make such a sound. Both slowly glanced beside them, to Myrna's room, where a shadow now blocked the light under the door.

Tim shot his sister a look that read, *See what you did?!*

Another creak came from behind them. They spun and saw a shadow, also under Lucille's door.

Tim's eyes widened and he whispered, "I thought Ma said she couldn't get outta bed."

Lilly nodded. "Yeah. Let's get out of here." She put an arm around her brother and quickly guided him to the stairs leading to the second floor.

While approaching the attic, both noticed in their periphery sunlight flooding its stairwell, blasting through an open door at the top of the landing. Tim kept moving but Lilly slowed to a stop, ducked aside, and peered up. Two small windows allowed light in, which erased ninety percent of the upper level's creepiness. How the door got opened was of little concern to Lilly. Instead, her curiosity fell to the stack of books flanking the top two steps. There were about a dozen hardbacks total, placed aside as if someone had been sitting on the highest step, reading them.

The excitement of getting a new book blindly overrode her suspicion. She climbed a few stairs and saw a little more of the attic, catching a large bookcase against the far wall, half covered by a dust sheet.

Although she wanted to rush in and check out the books lining the shelves, Lilly contained her excitement and crept back down to the hall to make sure they were still alone.

Tim's head and shoulders appeared over the horizon of the stairs leading down to the second floor. *C'mon!* he mouthed and quickly waved her over.

Lilly alternated glances between her brother, the sunlit attic, and the two doors belonging to the old women. Her eyes settled on the attic.

Just a quick peek. Scan their spines and grab something of interest, something she hadn't read before. Although the shelves probably wouldn't contain any young adult novels, there had to be a literary classic in the group. Maybe one from last summer's reading list. Surely there had to be a *Moby Dick, Treasure Island,* or *To Kill A Mockingbird.*

She waved Tim over to join *her.*

He shook his head. *Nuh-uh! No way!*

Come on, she mouthed and pointed to the attic.

Tim reluctantly climbed a few steps and peeked past her to make sure the bedroom doors were still closed. What his sister was asking went well beyond the permission their mother granted earlier. They could get in big trouble for playing around up there. Even worse for going in the attic.

Lilly read his concern and dismissed it with an eyeroll. "Fine," she said in hushed tones. "Then c'mere and stand watch."

Tim shook his head again.

"*Please.* I'll only be a second. Promise."

A long moment passed before Tim caved. He darted across the hall and into the attic stairwell, reuniting with his sister. Both glanced up.

"See, they got windows up there," Lilly said. "Not so scary, right? Now you coming?"

"Nuh-uh!"

"Come on! We can explore together. I bet Shirley has a ton of cool old stuff up there."

"No. We can get in a lot of trouble. Ma will kill us."

"Oh, stop it. We can say we heard something and went to investigate."

Tim stared up the steps. "Aren't you scared? I mean, what about. . ." He thumbed in the direction of the two rooms next door.

"If we were bugging them, they would've come out by now and yelled at us. We just gotta be quiet and they'll never know."

Tim chewed his lower lip to hide the fact it was trembling.

"Okay, fine," she said. "I'm going. Gonna take a quick peek at what's on the bookshelf up there." She stepped forward and Tim grabbed her arm.

"Don't leave me."

"Then come with."

"Nooo."

"Oh, don't be such a baby." She yanked free of his sweaty grasp. "Lilly! Don't. Please. You're gonna get us in trouble."

By the time he finished his plea, she'd crept halfway up the stairs.

At the top of the landing, she peered inside and slowly entered, drawn to the bookcase.

From below, Tim watched her attention suddenly veer elsewhere, causing her to move deeper into the attic and out of sight. Bouncing with nervous anticipation, he waited for Lilly to reappear. Afraid of both leaving her alone and being left alone, he climbed one step and then another, hoping to catch sight of his sister. Two additional steps and he was a third of the way there. A little more of the attic came into view. A white sheet covered something bulky like a large piece of furniture. Above it, a pair of small arched windows stared back at him like disapproving eyes.

He climbed another step and froze, his eyes catching movement at the sliver of space along the door's hinge jamb. Someone stepped forward, creeping in from behind the door. Whoever it was must have been patiently waiting for the girl to enter.

Before they could reveal themself, the door started to creak shut, causing a shadowy wave to slide down the stairwell, enveloping Tim.

He stood rooted in fear. It couldn't have been Lilly closing the door since she disappeared in the opposite direction. He wanted to call out. Warn his sister someone was up there with her. Or go get his mom. She'd be furious at them, but Lilly's safety was worth more than getting yelled at.

Before he could do either, the creak of footsteps came from the other side of the wall, in the direction Lilly headed.

There was a shuffling sound, heavy footfalls. His sister's shriek of terror. A loud thud. Then silence.

A second later, the door slowly creaked back open by itself, inviting Tim to enter. Investigate. Daring him to rescue his sister.

After the door came to a stop, a slow, wispy exhale floated down, and a ghastly voice whispered, "Timmmmmmmm . . ."

His face twisted in a mask of terror. He screeched and raced down the steps, refusing to look back . . . even as heavy footsteps descended the attic stairs over his shoulder, rapidly giving chase.

FIFTEEN

KENZIE WAS GOING TO KILL Lilly if the young girl was playing another joke on her brother. She'd given them permission to go to the third floor for chores only, not exploring. Although she'd been guilty of the same offense only days earlier, Kenzie now understood such indiscretion could jeopardize their stay. Family or not, Shirley had every right to kick them out if they were disturbing guests or, more so, tenants.

She was polishing the living room coffee table when Tim flew down the stairs, bug-eyed and screaming as if pursued by the devil himself. By the time he could explain what it was all about, the commotion had drawn Shirley from the laundry room.

As they all made their way upstairs, Kenzie tried to read Shirley's temperament. The grave concern on her face was hopefully reserved for Lilly's welfare and not over the disturbance complaint she was bound to get.

Reaching the third floor, Kenzie, with Tim by her side, quickened her pace and made a beeline for the attic stairs. In their haste, both failed to notice Lucille's door slowly closing. Only Shirley caught it, which caused her to do a double take and pause slightly before continuing to more pressing matters.

Kenzie rushed into the attic and called for her daughter. The small arched windows thankfully provided enough light to safely maneuver the ghostly maze of draped furniture and boxes. In the far corner, an open door appeared to lead to a smaller room, possibly used for additional storage. Kenzie sped around the twists and turns of each aisle to reach it. Halfway there, she suddenly slid to a stop across the dusty floor.

Blocking their path was an old woman kneeling on the ground. She hovered over Lilly, who was lying on her back, staring up in a daze.

With the woman's gray hair obscuring her face, Tim sucked in a breath at the all too familiar sight and slid behind his mother for protection.

"Oh, geez," Kenzie said, rushing to Lilly's side.

Tim kept his distance, peeking out from behind a cluster of boxes.

The old woman looked up, and Kenzie was taken aback by an intense pair of icy blue eyes. "Best not to move her," the woman told Kenzie. Then she called to Shirley, who was quickly approaching. "Fetch me an ice pack and a wet washcloth."

Kenzie couldn't help but stare at the woman's slightly masculine face, lined with so many wrinkles it looked like a crumpled piece of tissue paper.

"Is the child okay?" Shirley said.

"She'll be a whole hell-of-a-lot better if you go fetch what I asked. Now hop to it, girl!"

Shirley nodded and quickly left.

Kenzie noticed the bulging knot along her daughter's hairline and tried not to panic. "Baby? You okay?"

Completely serene, Lilly appeared mesmerized by the other woman and ignored her own mother.

"Lilly. Hey," Kenzie said, vying for her attention. "Are you okay?" Still not receiving a response, Kenzie moved to block her daughter's view, forcing the girl to look at her.

Lilly's lids fluttered. "Ma?"

Kenzie gently cradled the girl's head. "What happened?" When Lilly didn't respond, Kenzie turned to the old woman for an answer and found her leaning far too close. Kenzie swore she was being smelled and immediately pulled back in unison with the woman, who cleared her throat and made the odd gesture of tapping her thumb to ring finger three times on her left hand.

"I was going through some of our crap in storage." She hitched a thumb over her shoulder to the small side room across the way. "Guess the girl thought she was alone until she saw me. Then she turned and ran smack dab into that," she pointed at a wooden column a few feet away. "Bounced off the damn thing like a pinball at full tilt and hit the floor."

"Lilly, honey," Kenzie said. "Are you okay?"

The old woman reached for the girl, paused, and pulled back. "By the way, I'm Myrna. I'm a nurse. Live in room Three-A. You mind if I give her a look-see?"

"No. Please do."

"Lilly, I want you to follow my wrinkled old finger. And just because it looks like a piece of beef jerky don't mean you can gnaw on it, okay? Now, move only your eyes, not your head. Got it?" Myrna waved her bony index finger back and forth in the air. It took a few swipes before Lilly locked in on it and did as she was told.

"Should we call nine-one-one?"

Myrna didn't respond, she was occupied monitoring the girl's pulse at the wrist. Kenzie repeated the question and Myrna continued ignoring her.

"Is she okay?" Kenzie asked impatiently.

Myrna finally answered, "Yep. She's a scrappy lil' squirt. She'll be fine."

Lilly felt the knot on her head and hissed.

"Ooah, hurts when you touch it, don't it?" Myrna asked.

Lilly nodded.

"Well, if it hurts when you touch it, then don't touch it, silly."

Kenzie exhaled. "God, Lilly. You scared me half to death." She turned to Myrna. "Can we move her? Get her downstairs?"

"Not yet."

"Why? Too dangerous?"

"Not for her. My knees are shot to shit and I heard something pop when I knelt to help her. Now I'm afraid to stand up. Think I need a minute or two."

"Oh, God. I'm sorry."

"Don't be. Just give me a hand when I gotta get up and we'll call it even. Until then, we'll get ice on that knot and let her get her bearings back, then bring her down."

Heavy footfalls traveled up the stairs. Shirley finally appeared, completely gassed, but carrying the items requested earlier.

"'Bout time," Myrna mumbled.

After handing Myrna the Ziploc bag of ice and washcloth, Shirley stepped behind Tim and placed her hands on his shoulders. Finding the boy stiff as a board, she gave him a comforting pat and squeeze to reassure him everything was all right.

Myrna applied the ice to the knot, which elicited another hiss and a hearty shiver from Lilly. "Oh, you're fine. Suck it up."

Kenzie took the damp washcloth, folded it lengthwise, and gently held it over her daughter's brow. After an awkward silence, she addressed Myrna. "I'm really sorry for the inconvenience. I know you have enough on your plate. Hope we didn't disturb the other woman downstairs."

Hearing the reference to Lucille, Myrna locked eyes with Kenzie. "Oh, don't worry about her none. Most of the time that old bat sleeps like the dead."

After holding her stare a few moments too long (with those eerie blue eyes), the old woman smiled, unsheathing yellow, gapped teeth.

~

"Should we take her someplace to get checked out?" Kenzie asked, gnawing on her fingernail.

Shirley stood in the bedroom doorway, observing mother and daughter while Myrna sat on the edge of the mattress, tending to Lilly. Tim knelt on the opposite side of his own bed, eyeing Myrna suspiciously as she waved a penlight back and forth in his sister's face.

"Maybe she needs an x-ray or something?" Kenzie continued. "Just to be sure."

Myrna shrugged. "That's your prerogative. Go right ahead if you don't trust my opinion."

"I didn't mean that you're not qualified to—"

"Oh, it's only a bump, right?" Shirley asked.

Myrna nodded and clicked off the penlight.

"A hospital will charge an arm and a leg for a lot of unnecessary x-rays," Shirley said. "Plus, the nearest one is forty minutes away."

Myrna turned and oddly gestured again, tapping her thumb and ring finger three times. "Don't advise travel."

"And half the way to it is by a bumpy dirt road," Shirley added.

Myrna exhaled, slightly annoyed. "The kid is fine. Just needs to relax and be still, especially now. So, let the girl rest."

Kenzie yielded. Lilly *was* looking much better. A little pooped, as expected, but still alert and responsive. And Shirley had a point about the costly x-rays, something Kenzie initially failed to consider. If both women thought a hospital visit was unnecessary, then maybe she was overreacting.

"If anything," Myrna continued, "it's a minor concussion. All she needs to do is rest and avoid straining her eyes for a few days." She addressed Lilly. "I hear you're big on reading. Lay off it for a while or you'll go permanently cross-eyed. Got it?" Myrna winked at the girl, patted her shoulder, then rose, wincing slightly over her bad knees.

"You sure you're okay?" Kenzie asked the old woman.

"Yeah-yeah-yeah, I'm fine. Look, regarding the squirt," she thumbed back to Lilly, "if it makes you feel better, I'll come down and check on her every few hours or so."

"Oh, I can't ask you to—"

"You don't have to. I'm a nurse. It's what we do."

"Well then yes, I'd *really* appreciate that. Thank you."

Myrna grunted and checked her watch. "I've gotta tend to Lucille now. I'll be down after six." She walked out of the room without another word.

Kenzie called out, "Okay. Thanks, Myrna. Thank you!"

Failing to get a response, Kenzie turned to Shirley and shrugged over the awkward exchange.

Shirley stepped closer and whispered, "Don't mind her none. Told you her social skills aren't the best."

"I feel really bad about this. Since we've been here it's been nothing but drama. I mean, first with Tim the other night and now—"

Shirley waved her off. "Stop it. You're family. It's what we do for one another. Now, Come on. Let's go downstairs so the child can rest."

"Okay. I'll be down in a second."

"Tim, how about you come help me choose the menu for dinner tonight?"

Tim glanced from his sister to his mother then back again. He was being protective, not wanting to leave the girls alone.

That's my little man, Kenzie thought. "Go on. Go help Shirley. It's okay."

The boy slid off the bed and accompanied Shirley downstairs.

Kenzie scooted closer and carefully brushed her daughter's bangs aside. "How you doing, kiddo?"

Feeling her mother's comforting touch, Lilly nestled deeper into the pillow. "Okay. I guess."

"You know you shouldn't have gone in the attic, right?"

"I was only trying to find something new to read. That's all. I didn't get us in trouble, did I? Is Shirley mad?"

"Not sure. But I know you gave us all quite a scare. Guess Myrna gave you one first, huh?"

The girl looked confused.

"Myrna said she scared you. Did you not see her up there?"

"Ma, I didn't see her until you guys came up with her."

Kenzie chuckled, but there was no humor in it. "What are you talking about? She said she accidentally scared you and you tried to run away. That's when you ran into the pole and hit your head."

"Wha? All I remember is going to the attic, looking around at the bookcase, then waking up and seeing you guys over me."

Kenzie's brow furrowed. "That's all you remember?"

"Yeah."

"You sure?"

"Yes."

Kenzie paused. *See, now this,* this *I don't like.* She'd have to point out the sudden memory loss to Myrna when seeing her later. Make sure it wasn't anything serious.

"My throat kinda hurts," Lilly said. "Can I have something to drink?"

Earlier, Myrna placed a full glass of water on the nightstand. Kenzie grabbed it. "Drink slowly."

Lilly nodded, took the water, and gulped it down.

~

Shirley and Tim jolted when the door ripped open.

On their way to the kitchen, they nearly collided with Ben as he exited his room.

Appearing equally startled, he quickly stepped back into his doorway and used his body to block their view inside. "Is everything all right? I heard a commotion upstairs earlier." He seemed more nervous than concerned.

"I'm sorry we woke you," Shirley said, even though it appeared he hadn't been asleep.

"Oh, no problem. Is everything okay?"

Shirley peeped over his shoulder and into the room. His large bag was zipped up tight and lying diagonally across the mattress, making it impossible for him to have been asleep on the bed. A quick glance down revealed he was still wearing his shoes, fully laced up.

Ben noticed her wandering eye and adjusted the door, so the

opening became a little tighter.

"Everything's fine," Shirley said, "And again, sorry if we woke you. There shouldn't be any more disturbances. Have you decided if you'll be joining us for dinner?"

He smiled. "Sure. I'd love to."

"Wonderful. As I mentioned earlier, it'll be served in the dining room at six."

"Sounds great. I'll see you then." He waited for them to move on.

It was only after they made it into the kitchen that Shirley heard Ben's door close and immediately lock.

~

Ben backed away from the door, went to the window, and stared out at the gravel driveway. His room's location couldn't have been better, acting as a perfect sentry post to keep tabs on who came and went.

Sitting in the chair by the sill, he rubbed his sweaty palms on his jeans, and peered beyond the glass to make sure they weren't about to have unexpected visitors.

SIXTEEN

AS PROMISED, DINNER WAS SERVED at six. Seated around the table were Ben, Kenzie, Shirley, and Tim. Throughout the meal, Ben joked with the boy and made him laugh in a way Kenzie could barely remember. For the first time in a long time, dinnertime with a man in attendance was a real joy. Meals back home were pretty much silent unless Paul initiated conversation, which completely depended on the type of day he had.

Thank God that was all in the past now.

After dinner, Kenzie brought up a tray with three plates of food. While dropping off Lilly's, she was informed by the girl that Myrna, being true to her word, had recently checked in on her. Once Lilly was propped up and eating, Kenzie told her she'd return after delivering the two remaining plates.

On the floor above, she briskly walked past the attic entrance. Lilly's incident up there earlier might've reduced its mystery, but it still gave her the creeps, especially with it being dusk, and how the sun was reduced to a lavender afterglow in the two small windows. She set the plates outside Myrna's door and quickly returned to her daughter downstairs.

Lilly seemed to be doing much better, gobbling up all her food and downing three glasses of water. Her thirst was a bit disconcerting but at least dehydration wasn't an issue. And, oddly enough, the knot on her head was now barely noticeable.

After tucking the girl in for the night, Kenzie poured herself a large glass of red wine to enjoy on the front porch, where a cool breeze awakened the windchimes and swayed the surrounding treetops. With Tim and Shirley watching television inside, Kenzie planned to relish the alone time after dealing with the stress of the past few days.

She plopped down in one of the overstuffed patio chairs at the far end of the porch, kicked off her shoes, tucked her legs under, and felt the cool, soft cushion against her bare feet. As she was about to take her first sip, the screen door opened.

"Mind some company?" Ben said, poking his head out and holding a glass a wine.

Not wanting to be rude, she forced a smile and waved him over. He seemed like a nice enough guy, but she really would've preferred the time to decompress. Now she felt obligated to be back on the clock in order to entertain their guest.

Ben sat on the chair next to hers and stretched his long legs. He placed his wine glass on the side table between them and fished out a cigarette pack from his shirt pocket. "Mind if I burn one off?"

She did, but said, "No. Not at all."

He offered her one. When she politely declined, he pulled out a cigarette with his lips, flipped open a Zippo, and fired it up. He took a long draw on the smoke, its cherry burning bright and casting his face in a warm, orange glow.

Feeling obligated to start the conversation, she said, "It's beautiful out, huh?"

He nodded and exhaled a stream of smoke. "Absolutely."

"I've never been this far out in the country before."

"Really?"

"Yep, I'm city folk." She waited for a routine follow up, such as asking where she was from, but was pleasantly surprised when he said, "Me too," and left it at that.

They sat in silence, enjoying the cool night air and chorus of crickets. She felt her body relax and sink a little deeper into the soft cushions, while another sip of wine warmed her chest.

~

Sitting on the recliner in the living room, Shirley heard Kenzie's laughter sift through the window screen. She glanced down at Tim, who was lying on the floor watching a movie, a comedy, of course . . . no more horror flicks for the boy!

Shirley leaned back in her chair and attempted to peek out the window. The fact that Kenzie had been out there with Ben for a good twenty minutes made her a little uneasy. She still couldn't quite put her finger on the young man's intentions. Being so handsome, there was no doubt he was trying to work his magic on Kenzie. Such an attraction was normal between two young people, but she hoped Kenzie remained professional and didn't partake in any carnal shenanigans under her roof. After all, Ben was a guest and only passing through.

A smile slowly crept across her face. Ironically, the whole scenario reminded her of another tenant that arrived for a brief (yet intense) stay some forty years back, when her oh-so-handsome Roman—

The front door opened. Shirley contracted into the chair and threw her attention back to the television. From the corner of her eye, she glimpsed Kenzie making her way to the kitchen.

A minute passed then Kenzie returned with an open bottle of wine. "What're you guys watching? And Tim, it better not be a horror film!"

He gave her a quick glance. "It's called *My Name is Bruce*. It's a funny kung fu movie. Everyone thinks this one guy is Bruce Lee, but he's not. Ma, it's awesome!"

Kenzie shook her head and chuckled. "If you say so."

Shirley smiled and gestured to the wine bottle in Kenzie's hand. "I take it you two are getting along out there?"

"Oh, yeah. We're gonna have one more glass then head to bed."

Shirley shot a playful look. It took a moment for Kenzie to pick up on it.

"Oh, God. No! I mean *separately*. Like him in his room and me in mine."

"What?" Shirley said, grinning smugly. "I didn't say anything."

"You didn't have to!" Kenzie laughed. "Geez. No! Just . . . no."

Shirley watched her leave. Once she heard the front door open and close again, the smile quickly dropped from the old woman's face.

~

Shirley made sure Tim brushed his teeth and tucked him in bed before retiring to her own room, leaving Kenzie and Ben to continue their conversation on the porch. By the time they emptied the bottle of wine, Kenzie had a good buzz going. She was slouched in her chair, head tilted back, staring out at the starry night. Ben was also relaxed, his stretched legs crossed at the ankles, one arm dangling with a lit cigarette wedged between two fingers.

The vibe between them was purely platonic. It had been a long time since she had a guy friend and it was a nice change of pace to relax and be herself. Ben definitely gave off a bad boy vibe, but what was underneath appeared genuine. Of course, she was far from the best judge of character, and maybe the wine was fogging her assessment, but he seemed sincerely interested in what she had to say. He was actually listening and not waiting for her to stop talking in order to go on about himself or, as Paul often did, simply cut her off.

At first, their conversation didn't stray beyond the general. While reaching to refill his glass, she, once again, caught him checking out the bruises on her arm. Thankfully, he minded his own business about the matter. She really wasn't up for a lecture or advice from someone who didn't know shit about her situation.

Instead, they gossiped about the two old women upstairs, in which Kenzie repeated the few tidbits revealed to her during training. Passing that along to Ben was unprofessional, but the alcohol loosened both her inhibitions and her tongue. Besides, it was a subject she'd been dying to share, using Ben as a sounding board, especially since he was a fellow outsider.

Like Kenzie, he found it odd that the women had not left the house in decades. And how there hadn't been any correspondence (packages or letters) delivered to or from the premises. They never made or received phone calls. Had no visitors. They lived in total isolation. Recluses, relying on Shirley as their sole connection to the outside world.

Suddenly realizing how much she revealed to a complete stranger, Kenzie grew nervous. If Ben let something slip in front of Shirley, a sense of betrayal would be more than justified, especially after all the kindness the woman showed Kenzie and the kids.

Maybe Paul's right . . . sometimes you can be a real idiot. A good for nothing, piece-of-shit that deserves to be—

"Hey, Kenzie?"

Ben's voice made her jump. Thankfully, he was too busy brushing cigarette ash off his shirt to notice.

"Can I ask you something?" he continued.

She squirmed in her chair, hoping it wasn't pertaining to anything about the house, its owner, or the guests. Far too much had already been said.

"Well, actually . . ." He cleared his throat and took a drag. "It's more of a favor."

"Okay. What's up?"

After confirming they were alone, he leaned in. "It's just . . . I don't mean to freak you out or anything, but . . . umm . . ."

His pause was drawn out way too long. Kenzie moved closer as Ben struggled to find the words, looking everywhere except at her.

"I kinda need my stay here to be kept on the down low. Especially if anyone comes around asking about me. Like . . . ah . . . oh, fuck it . . . like especially the cops. Okay?"

Kenzie leaned back and quietly sighed. Great. Once again, her judge of character had failed her miserably. Why was she a magnet to such bullshit? "What kinda trouble are you in?"

"It's not anything too serious. I mean *really* serious. I mean, it is. But—"

"What did you do?!" Kenzie was surprised she blurted it out. It was a given he was about to confess, but what if it was something like he murdered a family of five? And now that she knew about it, he'd have to kill her and everyone else inside. Maybe it was best she didn't know. But the question had already been asked. She slowly untucked her feet and planted them on the ground in case she needed to make a mad dash inside to lock him out.

Ben read her sudden fear. "Whoa-whoa-whoa-wait. I'm not dangerous or anything. Ya see, I got in a fight with a guy and hurt him real bad. And now the cops want me 'cause he's pressing charges."

Okay, Kenzie thought, *not as bad as I was expecting*. Still. "Why did you get in a fight with him?"

"Over a woman."

Kenzie almost rolled her eyes. So, Ben was actually a meathead. Still fighting over girls, huh? Nice.

"It happened a county over. A day and a half ago. I was passing through. Decided to stop and have a beer and check out the local scenery. So, I'm sitting at a booth, alone, minding my own business, when I hear a girl scream. Well, it wasn't like a scream from a horror movie or something, more like a yelp. A yelp of pain. It came from the back of the bar, by the pool tables. At first, I thought it was someone goofing around so I didn't turn and look. But then I heard it again. And this time it sounded a lot more urgent. More . . . fearful. Now I lean out of the booth and take a look back, and see some guy getting rough with this girl. Since they're the only two back there, I figure they're a couple or something, ya know? Anyway, he has her pinned up against the pool table, twisting her arm."

Kenzie slowly exhaled and tried to calm her racing heart over the all too familiar experience.

"The way he's got her pinned, they're both facing me. He's behind her, pushed up against her. And he's eyeing her up and down, really getting a kick out of how he's putting the fear of God in her. But she's staring ahead. Right at me. And I tell you, seeing that terrified look in her eyes . . ." He shook his head and gazed into the night for a moment.

Kenzie sat in silence, grateful for the pause. It gave her time to get her emotions in check.

"Now this bar, it's got plenty of locals. Probably more than a half-dozen guys, plus the bartender. Big guys. Way bigger than the asshole in the back getting rough with the lady. But none of 'em are doing shit. They're completely ignoring the situation after she screams again. Even louder. I look back at the couple and see the guy now has the girl bent over the pool table. Her arm is all twisted up behind her back, like he's about to snap it. And she's still looking at me, tears streaming down her face, *still* too afraid to call out for my help." He paused again, his jaw tightening.

"So . . . what happened?"

"Well, I got up and hurt him. Real bad. Broke his arm and leg. Knocked out a few of his teeth. Might've even broken his jaw."

"God."

"I told him to stay down, but he kept getting back up. Guess he thought I was trying to take his woman away. Or trying to save face in front of her."

"Was the girl okay? Did they call the cops?"

"Yeah, she did. But not on him. On me. For beating him up. Turns out she's his wife and he's the son of a guy that owns the biggest car dealership in the area. The little shit is a real Richie Rich. Guess Daddy runs the town and that's why no one was stepping in to stop Junior from hurting his missus.

"To most outsiders, it wouldn't make a lick of sense why the woman would call the cops on the guy who saved her from getting attacked, but Kenzie completely understood the girl's actions. Unless she was ready to leave him, there'd be hell to pay later if she didn't stand by her man, even if he had just served her a beating.

"Afterwards, I bolted back to my motel before the cops showed up. The next morning, I heard from some of the locals that Richie Rich was pressing charges against me, so it was time to get out of Dodge, which is kinda hard to do when you're on foot and have to stay inconspicuous *but* still ask around for a ride.

"On top of all that, it turned out it wasn't only the cops looking for me. Some of Daddy's goons almost caught me at a truck stop, but I managed to get away. That's when I figured it's best to lay low for a few days until things blow over. Make 'em think I'm already long gone, so they'll lower their nets." Ben scoffed. "I sure riled up a hornet's nest kicking junior's ass like that. Anyway, that trucker James was the guy that told me about this place. That's why I'm here. And that's why I'm asking for your discretion if anyone comes poking around asking questions."

After a long, deep breath, Kenzie said, "You don't have to worry about me. But to be honest, I can't speak for Shirley."

"Sure. Absolutely. But I only plan on sticking around for a day or two. Maybe if you could explain the situation to her and—"

"I'll see to it she agrees. Don't worry. Okay?" She crossed her arms and slid them tight across her belly. "You did the right thing. You stepped in to help someone in trouble when others wouldn't. It's the least we can do to pay it forward."

"Thanks, Kenzie. I really appreciate it. But like I said . . . a day. Two, max. By then, his goons will probably think I'm already long gone, and it'll be much easier to slip out."

Kenzie nodded. "Well, if it helps any, you're more than welcome to stick around longer. If you like. Whatever you feel is best."

"Okay."

They turned and silently stared out at the curtain of darkness, filled with all sorts of things more than likely staring back.

~

Luckily, the kids remained asleep when a tipsy Kenzie, checking in on them for the night, bumped their dresser and cursed out loud.

Ben's story, combined with the excessive alcohol, dredged up emotions which knocked the wind from her sails. Hearing about the abuse hit way too close to home. Yet, it acted as a good reminder to always remain vigilant, especially in the immediate future. She hoped the anger Paul had toward her and the kids would eventually smolder until he forgot about them altogether. Believing so helped tether the paranoia lurking in the back of her mind. At least temporarily.

He probably doesn't give two shits we're gone, she told herself while walking down the dark hallway to the kids' room. *Even with the money I took, he probably feels it was a fair enough trade. How he essentially dodged a bullet getting rid of a basket case and her two kids, right? So, relax.*

After making sure each child was tucked in, she kissed them both and crossed the hall to her room.

Halfway there, Kenzie paused and cocked her head. Faint voices came from atop the staircase around the corner. Straining to hear who was speaking, she crept to the bottom step.

It was Shirley. Although the actual conversation was inaudible, the old woman sounded upset. Angry. Someone else spoke. Female.

Myrna.

Attempting to eavesdrop, Kenzie climbed a step, then a few more until a stair creaked underfoot.

The conversation halted.

Kenzie froze, fearing retreat would give her away. But the alternative was to stand in the open like some idiot, completely exposed to anyone peering down over the railing.

She carefully crept backwards.

The wood creaked again.

She winced, then realized the sound wasn't her doing. Instead, it came from above.

A shadow slid across the balusters.

Kenzie cut her losses and high-tailed it back to her room on the balls of her feet. She silently closed her door and pedaled back through the darkness until her legs bumped the edge of the bed. While waiting to figure out her next move, her skin crawled over the primal fear of entering a dark space without first making sure somebody (or *something*) wasn't already inside.

Her hand reached for the bedside lamp but stopped short when a shadow blocked the hall light spilling under her door. She'd been followed.

Her throat clicked and spine stiffened.

While waiting for them to move on, Kenzie began formulating an excuse for her spying in case she was called out, whether by an immediate knock on the door or later over breakfast.

I heard a noise and went to investigate. I thought I heard someone call my name . . . Oh, shut up! You're acting like a damn idiot. So what if you went to see who it was? So what if—

The shadow disappeared, sliding in the direction of the stairs leading down to the first floor.

Kenzie remained still until an icy breath cascaded upon the back of her neck. Before she could process what was happening, her body erupted in goosebumps. Her eyes bulged, rattled in their sockets.

Whoever stood behind her inhaled sharply, as if smelling her. Then their cold breath slid away.

Kenzie squealed and lunged forward, simultaneously flipping the light switch on the wall with one hand while ripping open the door with the other.

She barreled into the hall, snatched a candleholder off a nearby accent table, and raised the pewter piece over her shoulder like a club.

Steeling herself to move closer, she peeked into the room.

Although it appeared empty, the closet door was wide open.

Had she left it that way earlier?

She debated whether to call down for Ben. Doing so would wake the entire house. She could run downstairs to fetch him but that meant leaving the kids alone up there and that sure as hell wasn't about to happen.

The anxiety rush was sobering. She gripped the candlestick tight and crept into the bedroom, toward the closet. Pausing a few feet from its opening, she craned her neck, snuck a glance into the small bathroom opposite her, and found it empty.

Kenzie threw her focus back on the closet. After a deep breath, she rushed in with the candlestick raised.

Except for clothes on a hanger, a trash bag of her belongings, and the thick carpeted floor mat, the small room was empty and, more importantly, void of any intruder.

Shaking her head, Kenzie exhaled and shut the closet door.

Okay. What the hell just happened?

Regarding the breath on her neck, either she was drunk and imagining things, or . . .

She glanced up and saw an air vent above the spot where she'd been standing earlier. Maybe Shirley flipped the air on. It was too cool outside for it, but . . .

Kenzie groaned and rubbed her brow.

Maybe drinking wasn't such a good idea anymore.

After all, staying sober and aware of her surroundings was more important than trying to numb any anxiety she had over their uncertain future.

SEVENTEEN

"You can't be serious?"

Shirley smiled and patted Kenzie's arm. "It's only for a few days. You'll be fine without me."

"But who's going to run the place while you're gone?"

"Why you are, dear. You know all there is to know about it. I'm so glad we had the opportunity to go over everything before I got the call last night."

Ten minutes earlier, Kenzie came downstairs in her PJs and bathrobe to help start breakfast when she noticed two suitcases in the entryway. Thinking it was a new arrival, she almost ran back upstairs to make herself more presentable. That's when Shirley stepped out of the kitchen and told her the news.

An old friend phoned in the middle of the night, informing Shirley she was sick and asking for help. Apparently, this woman, Nina, was a childless widow with no one to care for her. She begged Shirley to come stay for a few days, a week max, long enough for her to get back on her feet. Shirley didn't go into any detail about their relationship, but Nina must have been important enough for her to drop everything at a moment's notice.

Now that Kenzie was made aware of the situation, Shirley figured she'd get a head start and hit the road earlier than planned.

Kenzie felt completely blindsided. Sure, they only had three guests (one of which was leaving in a day or so) but that wasn't the point. She was terrified of taking on such a responsibility only to (somehow) let Shirley down. What if an unexpected issue arose, one they hadn't discussed during training?

"I left you Nina's number. Call day or night if you have any questions or concerns." Shirley motioned to her open notebook on the kitchen counter. "There's all the notes we went over about running the place if you need to review. It's already open to the page where the checklist is. I wrote Nina's number in red across the top." She pointed to a piece of paper taped to the refrigerator, "And posted it there as back-up."

Kenzie nodded feebly.

Shirley gathered a few last-minute items to fill her purse. "Oh, and one other thing . . ."

Great, Kenzie thought, *now what?*

"I think it's best if you stay in my room while I'm gone. You need to be able to hear any guest who might call or arrive in the middle of the night. The doorbell is wired to ring only in my room, and the phone is right outside its door. You won't be able to hear either from the room you're currently in."

But Shirley's room was on the first floor. Away from the kids. "Are you sure about this? I mean, are you expecting anyone?"

"No one in particular. But we really can't afford to turn away business right now. Please don't take this the wrong way, but my food bill alone has doubled since you and the kids have arrived. We could always use the extra cash to balance things out."

"Sure. Sure. I understand."

Shirley noticed Kenzie's ashen complexion. "Heavens, child. You're going to do fine. Now there's enough food in the pantry and fridge to last well over a week." She leaned close and whispered, "And there's a hundred dollars in the safe in case you need a delivery from town. Number to the grocery store is by the phone. You still have the combo to the safe, right?"

Kenzie nodded again. She'd memorized it and, as backup, had it written on a folded sheet of paper shoved deep inside an extra pair of tennis shoes in her closet.

"Good. Now, you already have the keys to everything. And all the numbers to the utility companies are in the rolodex up front." Shirley checked her watch, shook her head, and gave Kenzie a peck on the cheek. Kenzie slightly flinched at her touch.

"Okay, take good care of the place and I'll call you from Nina's when I arrive. I'll call the house phone since your cell is acting squirrelly. Probably be later tonight. But if it happens to be *too* late, I'll wait 'til morning." Shirley left the room, heading for the foyer.

Kenzie remained in the kitchen, nodding like some simpleton. Then she quickly caught up with Shirley and held the front door open as the woman shuffled out with her luggage. "Well . . . um . . . okay . . . drive safe."

"Will do. We'll talk tonight."

Minutes later, Shirley's 1991 Cadillac roared down the driveway and disappeared behind the trees. Kenzie stood on the porch, half expecting the car to pull back into view with the woman laughing hysterically and trying to say, "You should've seen the look on your face!"

It was hard to fathom that Shirley would trust Kenzie (family or not, they'd only known each other for a few days) with both her business and her livelihood at the drop of a hat.

She's kidding, right?

Kenzie stared down the driveway for a good five minutes until finally realizing it wasn't a joke. She breathed deeply, stepped inside, and glanced around the place as if seeing it for the first time.

The grandfather clock in the lobby read six twenty-two. People would be waking soon and expecting breakfast.

Okay. So, you're in charge now. You got this.

~

Her gut sank when Tim said Lilly didn't want to get out of bed because she wasn't feeling well. "What do you mean? Not feeling well? How?"

Tim shrugged. He appeared more interested in what his mother was making for breakfast.

She removed the frying pan of scrambled eggs from the heat and turned off the burner. "C'mon."

~

Kenzie entered the room and found Myrna already at Lilly's bedside.

"It's okay," the woman told Kenzie after seeing her concerned look. "It has nothing to do with her fall from yesterday. It's more like a cold. Or the flu." She held up a coffee mug. "Already gave her something for it. She said her stomach hurt, so I whipped up a lil' herbal remedy."

Kenzie grimaced at the pungent odor throughout the room. "Is that what that smell is?"

Myrna feigned confusion and stuck her nose inside the cup. "Maybe it's a little potent. I suppose."

Kenzie approached her daughter, who was propped up against pillows. "You feeling sick, honey?"

Lilly coughed and shrugged.

"Your tummy hurt?"

"Did. But Myrna gave me a drink and it feels better now." The girl really sounded congested.

Kenzie turned to Myrna. "You're sure this doesn't have anything to do with her fall yesterday?"

"Yes. I've never heard of any correlation between a bump on the head and the common cold."

Kenzie thought it over and scoffed. It was a little ridiculous. "Sorry. And . . . and thank you."

"No problem. But I recommend she stay away from solids for a while. Let her stomach settle." She tapped the mug. "This'll help with that."

Kenzie nodded and shivered. The window over her shoulder was open, its sheer curtains swaying gently in the breeze. The room felt fifteen degrees cooler than the rest of the house. How could it be so downright frigid in there when it wasn't even that cold outside?

"God. No wonder she's sick." Kenzie went to the window and closed it. "Who opened this?"

"Was wondering that myself," Myrna said.

"I didn't," Lilly added.

Tim shrugged. "Don't look at me."

Kenzie turned back to Myrna hoping for more of an explanation, but the woman only looked away and tapped her finger and thumb three times. "I heard a car leave earlier," Myrna said. "Did Shirley go into town?"

"Ah, no. She left to take care of a sick friend."

"Oh. For how long?"

"Don't know yet. Only a few days. Hopefully."

"Does that mean you're in charge now?"

Kenzie paused a moment. "Yes."

Myrna smiled. "Well, congratulations on your promotion." She rose and let Kenzie take her place at the girl's side.

"How you feeling, kiddo?"

Lilly sniffled and coughed. "Kinda crummy."

Kenzie felt her forehead. It was a little warm.

"She just needs rest," Myrna said. "I'll check on her later and give her more broth." Then she turned and left without saying goodbye.

Once they were alone, Kenzie glanced over at the window. It wasn't open last night, was it? She would've remembered something like that when she checked in on the kids. Then again, she was a little tipsy. "Lilly, honey. Are you sure you didn't open the window last night?"

"Yes." Then she sniffled again, pulled the covers up to her chin, and closed her eyes.

~

"Ma, I told ya I didn't open it."

Kenzie gave Tim two more slices of bread for the toaster. "Okay, I believe you."

Crackling bacon filled the silence as she tried to figure out who else would've opened the window.

Over her shoulder, Tim sneezed.

She saw him wiping his nose on his sleeve. Great. He better not be getting sick too, especially helping with food prep. Wouldn't it be perfect if her kids got everyone in the house ill on her first day left in charge?

She grabbed the disinfectant wipes from under the sink and handed them to Tim. "I'll finish breakfast. Take these and wipe down all the doorknobs and light switches on the first and second floors. And be careful, they have chemicals on them so once you touch 'em, don't rub your eyes or pick your nose until you wash your hands first. Okay?"

Tim nodded, turned to do as he was told, and almost ran into Ben, who entered the kitchen.

"Hey, buddy," Ben said, ruffling the boy's hair. Then he smiled at Kenzie. "Good morning."

"Good morning to you, too," Kenzie replied and looked past him. "Hey, Tim? Don't worry about wiping down the third floor. It's off limits from now on. Got it?"

"Got it," the boy said and left.

Kenzie knew he had no intention of going up there alone but needed to be crystal clear to avoid another incident.

"So, what can I do to help?" Ben said.

The toast popped up.

Kenzie shrugged. "Throw in two more slices."

~

And then there were three. The number of settings at the dining room table shrunk even more so since their last meal. With Shirley gone and Lilly trying to sleep off her cold, that only left Kenzie, Tim, and Ben.

After placing a breakfast tray outside Myrna's door, Kenzie did as requested and moved her few belongings down into Shirley's room. Ben offered to switch rooms with the kids, giving them his on the first floor in order to keep mother and children together. Kenzie would've accepted if not for Myrna's bad knees. It was inconsiderate to expect the old woman to climb up and down another flight of stairs during her routine checks on Lilly.

Maybe they'd switch once the girl got a little better.

~

While Lilly slept and Kenzie tended to chores, Ben and Tim tossed a ball out back before getting bored and exploring the tree line.

"What's that?" Tim said, pointing to a strange marking on the backside of an oak.

Ben stepped up for a closer look and saw a crude carving in a small area stripped of bark at the top of the trunk. The symbol looked like a diamond bisected by an inverted cross.

"Hey!" Tim said at the next tree over. "There's another one here." He pointed at the spot where two large branches separated from the trunk.

Again, the area was void of bark, providing a clean slate for the artist. This time, the symbol was an inverted triangle with a circle around it and a crude eye carved in its center. Sap, long since hardened, seeped from the inner corner of the eye like amber tears.

Ben and Tim stared at each other for a moment, then turned in unison to the next largest tree, located about ten yards down and much closer to the house.

Without another word, both raced over to check it out.

Like the others, it had an arcane symbol carved where the trunk and branches met. It was a crude hand with long fingers reaching up to a circle, possibly representing the sun or moon. Or hell . . . it could've just been a Frisbee for all Ben knew.

"These are cool. What are they?"

Ben didn't answer. Instead, he was referring to the previous trees, hoping to spot a pattern.

They were all large oaks sticking out along the tree line. He saw another across the yard and bet it also had a carving. To its left was a similar oak. And another to the left of that one. He was willing to go all in that the pattern continued to the front of the house, forming a perfect circle surrounding the inn.

"Ben? What are they? You think they're like really old? Like done by cavemen?"

"Nah." He stared at the tree in front of him. "Probably just some bored kid with a pocketknife who stayed here a long time ago. That's all, buddy."

~

Peering out the kitchen window, Kenzie watched Tim and Ben in the backyard. Whatever they were eyeing in the tree—squirrel, bird, lizard, or big-ass bug—couldn't be seen from her vantage point, but Tim appeared to be having a good time and that's what mattered.

She kept close tabs on them while doing chores, telling Tim beforehand to always stay within sight of the house. Ben seemed like a pretty standup guy, but he was still a stranger and Kenzie didn't want her son going off into the woods with him. Nowadays, it was too damn hard to tell who the creeps were.

You knew about Paul, yet that didn't stop you from moving in and exposing your children to him. His disgusting face, leering at little Lilly, flashed in her mind. Then rage flushed her chest.

No. Not anymore, she thought and finally took pride in having the strength to leave, especially since all roads led there.

And *there* seemed like a damn good place to be.

EIGHTEEN

THE FORECASTER WARNED A MASSIVE line of storms moving in the following night would not only wash out the remaining workweek, but possibly the entire weekend. There was also a high probability they'd prevent any chance of seeing the lunar event that was all the rage on the news the past few days. Something about a rare super blue blood moon, last occurring nearly a century ago. Kenzie thought it would be cool to watch something so unique, but with how intense things were supposed to get, she was more concerned about flooding. A long, wet one like the region hadn't seen in years was what the weatherman predicted. At least they had enough food in the house to easily wait it out. If Kenzie did have to drive somewhere in the thick of it, her Jeep Cherokee should be more than able to handle such a trek.

She kept the television on low while dusting the living room to provide a little white noise against the house's silence. The news stories, whether good or bad, reminded her life went on as usual and, contrary to how she felt sometimes out there in the boonies, they weren't the last people left on earth.

Of course, the weight of their isolation might not feel so heavy if she knew how close they were to town or even in which direction it lay. If her piece of crap cell phone would only get a signal, she could look up the answer.

Earlier, Shirley mentioned a grocery store that delivered, so it had to be reasonably close for them to offer such service.

A trip into town would be a welcome change. Take in new scenery, do a little browsing, and chase away any looming cabin fever. Surely the kids would appreciate something like that. They might even find a bookstore for Lilly and a toyshop for Tim. If so, she still had a few bucks left over for them to pick out something cheap.

But with Shirley absent, none of it was an option. They couldn't leave the house unattended, even for a few hours. What if a new guest arrived? Or something happened like, God forbid, Myrna fell down a flight of stairs because of her bum knees?

Nope. With Shirley gone and Lilly still sick, she and Tim would have to be patient and wait things out.

~

That night Tim vomited not only at the dinner table, but all over it. All over the lasagna dish Kenzie spent the afternoon preparing. And the hand-stitched tablecloth Shirley was so proud of. And nearly on Ben and Kenzie, if they hadn't leapt back in time to avoid the projectile of undigested food.

It was alarmingly sudden, like flipping a switch. Afterward, Tim slumped in his seat, his face pasty and white, cheeks huffing and puffing. A long ribbon of drool stretched from his chin.

Kenzie's first thought (besides *Holy shit!*) was food poisoning, but she and Ben were fine.

While she carried her son upstairs to put him down for the night, Ben was kind enough to clean up the mess. He rushed each plate to the garbage can, scraped it clean, rinsed it off, and stuck it in the dishwasher, all before the smell of puke got to him.

Upstairs, as Tim lay under the covers, Kenzie dabbed his sweaty forehead with a damp washcloth. "You feeling better, Timbo?"

Eyes closed, he slowly shook his head.

"Not even a little?"

He shrugged and opened his eyes but avoided hers.

"I know *I* always feel better when *I* throw up," she said. "It's how our bodies get rid of the crummy stuff really fast." She was trying to allow him to save face, knowing he was probably more than a little embarrassed about getting sick in front of his new pal Ben. "It happens to all of us."

After a moment, he finally looked at her. "Ma, I'm sorry 'bout ruining dinner."

"Oh, baby. It's okay."

"You think Ben's mad I barfed on him?"

Bingo. Still got it. "No. Not at all. You're sick. You couldn't help it."
She glanced at Lilly, sleeping peacefully one bed over. A coffee mug
sat on the nightstand beside her, one she didn't quite recognize from
the collection downstairs. "Probably got the same bug as your sister."

Kenzie moved to Lilly's side and felt the girl's forehead for a fever.
All seemed fine. And oddly enough, the knot was gone. Lilly stirred
but didn't wake when her mother brushed a wild hair from her brow
and pulled the covers up tight.

The mug on the nightstand drew Kenzie's curiosity. She picked it
up and sniffed inside. Nothing really smelled out of the ordinary, especially not like the funky scent filling the room earlier.

She studied the sleeping girl and suddenly felt an overwhelming
urge to prod her awake for verbal confirmation she was feeling better.

Would you relax and let her sleep?

Approaching footsteps sounded in the hall. Kenzie turned.

Myrna entered the room and headed in Lilly's direction with a
metal bedpan.

"Oh. I don't think that's necessary," Kenzie said, standing. "I can
take her to the bathroom."

"It's easier on everybody if she uses it." Myrna placed the pan on
the ground and, using her foot, slid it under the bed, out of sight.

Kenzie shrugged. "But I don't think she'll be able to go in it. It'll
be too awkward for her to—"

"She's already used it."

"Really?"

Myrna nodded. "I was just emptying it. She's fine with it." The
old woman turned to Tim. "Now what's the matter with this one?"

"He threw up at dinner."

"Food poisoning?"

"No. Ben and I ate the same thing and we're fine."

"Is it what you left at our door? What is it? Meatloaf?"

Considering her time spent preparing the dish, the question stung.
"Lasagna."

Myrna grunted. "Hard to tell with it smothered in so much gravy."
She reached down and felt Tim's forehead.

Dismissing the food critique, Kenzie focused on the kids. "Could
it be the flu? Or whatever Lilly has?"

Myrna glanced from Kenzie, down to her daughter, then back again. "Does kinda look like a bug is going around, don't it?"

Kenzie did a double take at Myrna. Was the woman trying not to smile? Before she could question it, Myrna tapped her finger to thumb three times, glided past Kenzie, and retrieved the empty coffee cup from the nightstand. "I'll whip up some more for the lil' puke over here," she said, referring to Tim. "Just keep him off solids until I say."

Kenzie blocked her exit. "Hold up a sec. I'm curious . . . what's in it?"

"It's an old concoction of mine. A little licorice root, elderberry, ginseng, tannis roo—"

"All-natural stuff?"

"Yes. Why?"

"Is it safe for them? Being so young and all?"

"Yes. It's fine. Or would you prefer something made in a lab with chemicals none of us can pronounce?"

Kenzie didn't like her tone but kept silent because the woman was a nurse, one that Shirley trusted. And although asleep, Lilly's breathing sounded less congested when compared to yesterday. Whatever she was using seemed to be working. "I only want what's best for my kids," Kenzie replied. "What's safest."

Myrna held up the mug and winked. "Good. Then I'll whip up some more for Tim."

~

As the sun dipped below the treetops, they stood on the edge of the porch and watched its warm, orange glow slowly fade. Kenzie checked over her shoulder to make sure they were alone, then resumed her conversation with Ben.

"There's something really off about her. It's like, she has zero social skills, so it makes her come off as a real bitch. And she's got this nervous tick. It sounds really shitty of me to say, but it kinda creeps me out."

"Why? What does she do?"

"Well, it's basically this weird thing where she taps her fingers together." Kenzie demonstrated and Ben laughed.

"Oooooah, so creepy!"

She chuckled too. "I know, I'm being stupid. I guess it's more awkward than creepy. But still."

"Ah, forget about her. What about Lilly? She doing better?"

"Yeah. She was so zonked out I didn't wanna wake her."

"Well, that's a good sign. I know whenever I get the flu, I gotta crash hard for like a day or two. Get all in a Nyquil-induced coma before I feel better. So, try to relax. I'm sure she'll be up and about soon."

Kenzie exhaled. Maybe Ben was right. Maybe it was the stress getting to her. They both stared at the sunset.

"Pretty, huh?"

Kenzie nodded. "We should enjoy it. The news said we're gonna get a ton of bad storms starting tomorrow night."

"I saw that. And it's gonna ruin our chance to see that super-duper blood moon eclipse thingy or whatever the hell it's called."

"Yeah, isn't it crazy how they're really hyping that thing?"

"Probably for ratings. They're trying to make it sound all spooky with that 'it last happened nearly a century ago' bullshit to get people to tune in."

"I guess. But the rain is supposed to be pretty much nonstop. Even into the weekend. Which sucks because I wanted to check out the hiking trail Shirley told me about. Was hoping to start running again to get a little exercise."

"You a morning or evening runner?"

"Usually mornings. Before breakfast. But, hell, I'd do evenings just to be able to burn off some calories and not feel like such a porker."

Ben nodded and looked away. "Rain for a few days, huh? That sucks. It's gonna be a long walk back to the road for me if it's pouring."

"Well, I could give you a ride." She immediately regretted the offer. First, it meant she'd be leaving her sick kids alone at the inn, even if it were for only a half hour there and back. Also, she enjoyed Ben's company and didn't want him to leave.

"Nah. I couldn't ask you to do that. Besides, maybe I'm not ready to go yet. I know I really should be getting out of Dodge, but it's peaceful here." He flashed a warm smile. "And the people are nice."

Kenzie blushed slightly. "Well, you're more than welcome to stay. It's nice having you here."

Ben nodded. "Yeah. We'll see. Think I'll sleep on it."

~

Both kids were tucked in tight, and Tim had recently downed Myrna's herbal remedy. Kenzie caught him before he fell asleep, unlike Lilly, who was already zonked out with a smile on her face.

"How you feeling?" she asked him.

"Sleepy."

Kenzie whispered, "Hey, how was Myrna's drink?"

"Kinda gross."

"Yeah?"

Tim nodded.

"But did it make your tum-tum feel better?"

Another nod, then a yawn.

She kissed his forehead. "Okay. Get some sleep and you'll feel better in the morning."

Tim closed his eyes and smiled. Kenzie got up and gave Lilly a kiss, then exited the room. Retiring downstairs for the night, she left their door half open in case either kid called out for her.

Thankfully, Myrna planned to check on them in the middle of the night. The old woman might be odd, but Kenzie was grateful for having essentially a live-in nurse on call, twenty-four-seven, free of charge. Given the situation, things could not have been any more convenient.

Once downstairs, Kenzie entered the master suite and saw it was already nine fifty-three and Shirley had yet to call. Although her cell phone on the dresser had no missed calls, it didn't have any signal bars either. Before assuming the worst, she remembered Shirley saying if she reached her destination too late, she'd call in the morning. Kenzie figured that was the case and put her concerns to rest for now.

Leaving her bedroom door open to listen for the kids, she debated if it was really necessary to stay downstairs. What were the odds of someone showing up in the middle of the night to rent a room? Highly unlikely, but it was probably best to respect Shirley's wishes.

Kenzie plopped onto the bed and stared at the ceiling. With all the lights off on the first floor except for the one in her room, darkness hung like a black velvet curtain outside her door.

Maybe she *would* sleep upstairs to be closer to the kids. Just for tonight. No one was going to show up.

Then again, Ben had arrived out of the blue. Maybe the trucker who sent him their way was currently recommending the place to someone else. So maybe it was best to stay put.

The hardwood creaked outside her room.

Kenzie sat up and stared ahead.

"Ben?"

No reply.

She stepped into the hall and flipped on the nearest light, illuminating the foyer. A quick peek down the corridor showed Ben's door was closed.

Her focus shifted to the living room, where the darkness was so thick it could easily conceal someone standing out in the open, right in front of her. She gazed into the void and the fine hairs on her arms prickled.

A toilet flushed somewhere in the other room behind her.

She sucked in a breath and spun around.

As the water flowed to the septic tank out back, the pipes rattled loudly between the walls.

Kenzie scoffed, shook her head, and gave the living room a cursory glance. "It's an old house. Full of weird noises. Better get used to it."

She flipped off the foyer light and shuffled back inside her suite to use the restroom.

Once her bathroom door was shut, the house fell silent until a slow, rhythmic breathing resumed within the living room's darkness.

~

After brushing her teeth and changing into her PJs (a large t-shirt draping her tiny frame), Kenzie lay in the dark and stared at the ceiling. Her thoughts soon returned to Shirley's welfare. The woman was probably too busy tending to her friend to call. And after a long trip like that to . . .

It dawned on Kenzie she never bothered to ask where Nina lived. *Because you were too freaked out about being left alone and in charge. Way to go, stupid!*

Before berating herself any further, she exhaled and pushed it aside. She needed to stop being so hard on herself. Choice words from a former co-worker rang clear in her mind: *"Hon, it's all that negativity you keep bottled up that'll only attract more of the same."*

It summed up her slew of relationships, including those with the fathers of her children (and how Paul managed to slither his way into her life). She'd always been attracted to bad boys. Always sought some sort of warped challenge with first trying to win them over, then change them. But it was time to grow up. She was rather proud of the fact that, although finding Ben attractive, she refused to pursue things any further.

Right now, she needed a friend, and his actions back at the bar the other night proved one thing . . . that he was one of the good guys.

~

The cash and jewelry Ben stole over the past week was staggering. Before removing the items from his duffle bag and placing them across the bed for a quick inventory, he made sure the curtains were drawn tight, then triple-checked the lock on the bedroom door.

His winning streak of burglarizing farmhouses came to a screeching halt only a few days ago. As with his previous scores, Ben scoped out the property and thought its homeowners, an old man and his wife, left together. Although he'd seen their pickup pull out of the garage and disappear down the long winding road, he didn't witness them both getting into the cab. When the truck drove away, the window tint was too dark to make out the number of occupants.

He waited to be certain no one was home, but grew impatient— or more so, reckless—and decided to take a chance.

Stashing his duffle bag in the weeds to lighten his load, he slid on a ballcap and into the part of the unfortunate traveler, one searching for a phone after having car trouble miles away. Ben knew it was a silly scenario, but with no one supposedly being home, it wasn't something he expected to be called out on.

With only a screen door barring entrance, he rang the bell, waited, then peered inside through the fine wire mesh.

No response.

He rapped on the doorframe and called for any occupant, but still received no reply.

After a quick check of his surroundings, he pulled the bill of his ballcap down and tried the door. When the handle wouldn't turn, he sliced the screen with a pocketknife, reached through, and unlocked it. The rusted spring attached to the door twanged and popped as it stretched open.

Once inside, he glanced around the living room and kitchen before moving to the master bedroom. He found nothing under the mattress but, nevertheless, felt for any cuts or tears along its side where something might've been secretly inserted.

It was amazing how predictable people were when it came to their valuables. Jewelry was always left out on nightstands, the sink, or atop the dresser. Cash? Usually hidden under the mattress or at the back of an underwear drawer. Or possibly crammed in a shoe box under the bed, a ratty pair of cowboy boots in the closet, or an empty coffee can in the kitchen cabinet. Some people got a little more creative, such as beneath a loose floorboard (usually surrounded by tell-tale pry marks), an empty vegetable box in the freezer, or a Ziploc bag duct-taped to the back of the toilet tank.

Ben was cruising around on autopilot when the old man, clutching a double-barrel shotgun, stepped out of an adjacent room.

"What the hell you doin' in my house?!" Given his bloodshot eyes and bedhead of white hair, he appeared to have just woken from a nap. Even more apparent was the fact he didn't leave in that goddamn truck with his wife.

Ben didn't know if the man's extreme volume was out of anger or because of the large hearing aid stuck behind his ear like a giant wad of Silly Putty. In any case, he tilted his head down so the bill of his hat concealed as much of his face as possible. Then, peeking out from under its brim, Ben slowly raised his hands and hoped none of the stuff he'd already snatched was hanging out of his pockets. "Whoa-whoa-whoa, old timer. I knocked on the door, but no one answered. So, I—"

"Huh?!"

Ben really didn't know where he was going with the story, one which could justify entering the man's house without permission. But he was grateful for the do-over. "I said my car broke down and—"

"What?!" The old man narrowed his eyes and jabbed the gun at Ben like it was a spear. "Speak up!"

Jesus Christ, why even bother comin' up with something? The old bastard can't hear it anyway. Ben used it to his advantage and spoke softly, trying to lure the man closer. Only a few inches or so.

"I said that I . . ." and then he proceeded to mumble.

The man fell for it and took a step forward, craning his neck.

Ben lashed out and grabbed the barrel, knocking it away and pinning it against the wall. The gun bucked, simultaneously letting off a deafening boom, and the sheetrock exploded.

Tilting his head down and using the cap's bill as protection, plaster chunks and wood splinters blew past his face. "Goddammit!" Ben screamed. Caught in the heat of the moment, he instinctively swung back and threw an elbow at the old man's temple.

The blow was a direct hit, snapping the man's head to the side. His limbs turned to jelly, and his fingers loosened on the gunstock.

As his knees unhinged, Ben caught him by the shirt and gently lowered him to the hardwood floor. He cracked open the double-barrel and pulled out the unspent shell, throwing it one way and the gun, the other.

After catching his breath, he knelt to check on the man, terrified the elbow strike might've killed him. He found a strong pulse and gushed in relief. The poor bastard would probably wake with one hell of a headache, but he'd live. Ben turned him on his side in case he vomited while still unconscious, then placed a pillow under his head for comfort and left him lying in the hall.

Because things had gone so awry, Ben cut their phone line to prevent a call to the police, while also giving him a head start on his escape. He bolted from the house, retrieved his duffle bag, and kept to the backroads to stay out of sight.

After crossing county lines, he hitched a ride with a trucker named James Cooper. Something about the man was off, but upon noticing Ben's nervous reaction to a state troopers' roadblock up ahead, he turned his truck around without saying a word. Then he told him about the inn, and how it was a good place to stay since it's off the beaten path. Ben didn't know why the guy did what he did, but he sure was grateful for the break.

The roadblock must've been for something else. The small amount of cash and jewelry he had stolen on his spree could've easily been blamed on local kids. It never would've warranted something involving state troopers. But he wasn't about to take any chances, especially after violating parole a week earlier while crossing Florida's state line.

Luck had been on his side when picked up by the trucker who didn't question his suspicious behavior at the roadblock. And it continued after seeing the faded bruises on Kenzie's arm. It was just the info he needed to win over her trust by concocting some bullshit story about defending an abused woman at a bar. Being nice to her boy was added insurance, although the kid was pretty cool. Kenzie was too, but he wasn't looking to make friends.

Ben had his own kid to get to, a daughter on the west coast with a raging druggie for a mother. Reaching little Evie became his self-appointed rescue mission, one funded entirely by whatever he could steal. It was all to get Evie back, safe and secure and away from his bitch ex-wife before she or any of the shitbag friends she ran with harmed the girl.

He stared at the valuables on the bed and sighed. It wasn't enough for him and his daughter to begin a new life together, but it was a good start. With the tidbits gathered last night from Kenzie's loose lips, he knew the old bats were paying rent every month with cash. Which meant they must have a large stash of it somewhere up there.

The approaching storm would provide good cover, its thunder masking any noise he might make. He just had to wait for the right moment when Myrna was busy then sneak into their rooms and find where they kept the cash.

NINETEEN

"WHAT THE HELL ARE YOU doing in here?" Kenzie asked.

The smile dropped from Ben's face. "What? I-I hope it's okay." He flipped the omelet to prevent it from burning. The orange glow of the breaking dawn spilled through the window over his shoulder. "I know the kids are restricted to that broth diet, but that doesn't mean we have to starve, right?"

On the counter next to him was a stack of toast, freshly squeezed orange juice, and a tray set for the tenants on the third floor.

"Ben, you're a paying guest here. You're not supposed to be cooking for us."

Moments earlier, while still garbed in her jammies and slippers, Kenzie stepped from her room to go upstairs and check on the kids when the aroma of coffee and toast lured her to the brightly lit kitchen. Her initial thought was Shirley returned home early for some reason. But to her surprise, Ben was preparing breakfast. The only thing more enticing than the food's smell was the fact he was wearing a tight tank top flaunting his broad shoulders, solid chest, and chiseled arms. Her first reaction was almost "Whoa" instead of "Hey."

Kenzie went to switch places with him at the stove, but he held up his hand.

"Nope. I got this." He smiled. "Now's your chance to go for that run. Check out the trails you've been wanting to see. Before the storms move in, remember?"

She sighed. "What I said last night wasn't a hint for you to—"

"I know. I just couldn't sleep so I got up and took the liberty of starting breakfast. No biggie. Now are you gonna go for that run or stand there and ruin my good deed for the day?"

"You're serious?"

He nodded.

"You sure?"

"Yes! Go!"

"Okay-okay! But I wanna peek in on the kids first."

~

Kenzie opened the door and poked her head inside. Both Lilly and Tim were warm and secure in their beds, sleeping peacefully. All seemed fine.

Not wanting to forfeit the opportunity presented by Ben, she decided against waking them. She'd do so after her run and maybe, if it were okay with Myrna, bring them up some toast and OJ.

Before closing the door, her eyes caught the two coffee mugs sitting on the nightstand. Whatever the concoction was, she'd have to ask for the recipe.

Again, Kenzie felt extremely grateful to have Myrna there. Maybe once Shirley returned and the kids were feeling better, they'd drive into town and buy her a little something to say thank you. It wasn't lost on her that she really knew nothing about Myrna—her likes, her hobbies.

Well, all in due time, she thought. Something would be revealed.

~

While Kenzie stretched her legs on the back porch, Ben came out with a dish towel slung over his shoulder.

"Oh? You change your mind about joining me?" Kenzie said.

"Nah. Weights are more my thing. Besides, I already put on another omelet. Breakfast should be ready by the time you get back."

"Okay. I won't be long."

She was slightly hesitant about leaving him there alone, but things felt right with Ben. Besides, it would only be for about twenty minutes. Supposedly the trail circled the property, with the house plainly visible for most of the way. If trouble arose, she'd be within earshot and could easily dart back.

Things would be fine.

As Kenzie stepped off the porch, Ben scanned the thicket of trees out back. "Hey? How about this for protection. Just in case." He offered her the small club by the backdoor used to beat dust from the hallway runners and area rugs.

"Protection against what?"

"Coyotes. Stray dogs. Feral hogs. Bobcats. Bloodthirsty inbreds with a hankering for human flesh. Take your pick. Heard they've all been known to roam these parts. Remember, this isn't the city. Lots of wild animals out here."

"Well, we city folks can handle ourselves just fine, but . . ." Kenzie accepted the club and sized it up. "It'll be a good substitute for a set of hand weights."

"There ya go. Think of it as a five-pound dumbbell."

Kenzie strode halfway across the yard and pointed the stick at Ben. "I'll be within earshot, so holler if you need me for any reason." She gave a final wave and stepped onto the trail, picking up her pace until eventually disappearing behind a clump of trees.

Ben waited a minute in case she returned for whatever reason.

When she didn't, he rushed back inside and slid the frying pan off the hot coil, shut off the burner, and darted out of the kitchen.

~

The woods pressed tightly against the trail. The morning sun barely penetrated the dense canopy of leaves. What did cast harsh beams down to the forest floor.

While running, Kenzie swung the stick back and forth like it was a sword. Her labored breathing and clunky steps reminded her how out of shape she was. Trying to find a rhythm between lungs and legs seemed to be damn near impossible. Of course, the extra action with the stick wasn't helping matters, so she folded her arms close to her ribs and let them saw back and forth.

With each step, her heavy breathing muted her surroundings. Her heart wanted to punch its way out of her chest. There was no way she'd be able to keep up such a pace. It was a mistake to start off so hard and fast, instead of gradually increasing her intensity. Her calf muscles were tight. Cramping. She hadn't stretched nearly long enough.

Oh, forget this!

Kenzie slowed to a stop and gasped for air as if she'd sprouted gills and was thrown ashore. Dropping the stick, she shook out her legs and bent over to stretch her calves. With palms flat on the ground, she stared upside down through her legs and into the woods behind her.

Her eyes slowly rack focused like a camera lens, shifting from foreground to background. In the distance, someone (seen only in silhouette) was crouching on a log, watching her.

She gasped, sprung up and around. In the second it took to complete the action, the person had vanished. Far ahead, squawking birds took flight. Goosebumps rippled across her skin. She scanned the woods, noting the numerous areas of thick brush and large trees someone could easily hide behind.

Kenzie watched and waited for some confirmation she wasn't alone. But with each passing second, doubt crept in. Had she imagined it? Disorientation from being upside down while stretching? A trick of light and shadows?

No.

She felt their presence. And there was no way her jumping up from the stretch disturbed those birds, over a hundred feet away. Proof enough someone else was out there.

She rewound the moment in her head before the details faded. The figure glimpsed was odd. A dark silhouette—long and spindly yet human in shape. It balanced on the log, squatting with its arms planted firmly in front and head bowed.

Almost like a cathedral gargoyle.

Whoever or whatever it was didn't matter now, only that it was time to leave.

Keeping her eyes locked ahead, she retreated a few steps, then something grabbed ahold of her hair from behind.

Kenzie screamed, whirled, and swung at her attacker.

Her fist swiped the overhanging tree branch entangling her hair, ripping out strands at the root as she jerked her head away. "Oww! Jesus!"

There was no attacker, only her clumsiness from not looking where she was going. She rubbed her scalp and stomped her foot. "Shit! Fuck!" It hurt like hell.

Behind her, a branch snapped. She spun around but saw nothing.

As the hair slowly rose on the back of her neck, Kenzie snatched Shirley's club off the ground and raised it, ready to strike.

Fight or flight?

The answer was obvious, so the real debate became more about which way to run. If she chose to backtrack, the route she'd already traveled was choked by thick foliage, making it perfect for someone to lie in wait.

Ahead seemed much brighter from the sparseness of trees, but it was uncharted. Shirley mentioned how the trail eventually crossed the driveway somewhere between the main road and the inn. If she could reach the intersection, she could tear ass home down the drive and avoid blindly running deeper into the woods.

The crossing had to be close by.

As if her choice were all that difficult, the heavy footfalls across the forest floor, approaching fast and from the rear, decided her direction.

Refusing to look back, Kenzie turned and ran like hell for the crossing.

~

His plan worked flawlessly, and now he had the whole first floor to himself.

Ben figured the average jog for someone who hadn't done cardio in a while would take about ten to fifteen minutes before calling it quits. That would give him more than enough time to do a little reconnaissance behind the front desk.

Keeping a watchful eye on the stairs, he tried to open the wall-mounted key box, but found it locked tight. *All right, hold off on the room keys for now. What about cash?* He moved to the small safe under the counter. When the handle wouldn't turn, he methodically pressed zero on the keypad. After the fourth punch, the tiny light on its face flashed red. *Okay. It needs a four-digit combo.* He tried the obvious:

1-2-3-4

4-2-3-1

2-4-6-8

1-3-6-9

The light refused to turn green.

He continued punching random combinations, knowing damn well he'd have better luck winning the next lottery. So he circled back to the wall-mounted lockbox. The real jackpot had to be hidden in one of the third-floor rooms.

Ben rummaged through the drawers for a key to open the box. Upon checking in, he'd noted Kenzie used a keyring to unlock it. Which meant she probably left it behind while on her jog.

He looked out the front window, then back up the stairs. With the coast clear, he moved onto the master bedroom to continue his search.

~

Rocketing out of the thick foliage, Kenzie slid to a stop on the gravel driveway but found the house nowhere in sight. Fear and adrenaline threw off her sense of direction. Which way was home?

A branch snapped in the woods over her shoulder.

She spun and backpedaled a few paces. While her eyes ticked back and forth, searching for a threat, the swaying treetops caused shadows to dance within the woods.

Another crack. This time louder, making her jump as if hearing a gunshot.

She turned and started running. Her choice of direction was a split-second decision, one she hoped would take her back to the safety of the house and not in the opposite direction.

As she raced down the drive, branches cracked and leaves crunched in the woods to her left. Whatever was running along beside her was using the brush for cover.

Hearing its heavy breathing and crushing footsteps, Kenzie pushed her burning legs even harder to maintain the lead and, more importantly, prevent her pursuer from cutting her off up ahead.

~

Except for a few pairs of Kenzie's socks and panties, the top drawer of the dresser was empty. Ben tried the next one down and, finally, the third after that, but still found nothing. The keyring also wasn't under the mattress or box spring.

He entered the walk-in closet and stepped onto the thick carpeted mat, then ran a hand over the top shelf, sliding it underneath a stack of blankets until his fingers hit something hard and metallic.

Bingo.

He snatched up the keys and debated whether it'd be prudent to simply take them now.

No. Don't be reckless. It'll only make her suspicious if they go missing. She put them here for a reason. But now you know where she hides them.

He returned the keyring and smoothed the blankets to appear undisturbed.

Outside the room, the front door suddenly burst open and slammed shut.

Ben jumped at the commotion and shuffled deeper into the closet. After a moment, he inched forward and peered out between the door and the jamb.

Fast, heavy steps approached from down the hall, then someone whipped past the bedroom, heading for the kitchen.

Ben glimpsed a blonde ponytail.

Kenzie. *What the hell is she doing back so soon?*

~

Moments earlier, when the house appeared around the bend, Kenzie gushed in relief even as the stitch in her side knifed deeper and drew fresh tears. She leaped onto the front porch and shoved open the door, then spun on her heels and slammed it shut behind her.

Her trembling hands fumbled with both locks. She stumbled back and waited for a shadow to appear behind the door's curtain. For its handle to jiggle. For a pounding coming so hard from the other side, it would cause the door to throb in its jamb. Then for it to burst open in an explosion of splintered wood and broken glass.

But nothing happened.

She rushed to the side window overlooking the porch. Finding it vacant, her eyes immediately darted to the tree line encompassing the property. There was no sign of whatever had given chase.

She pushed away from the window and ran into the kitchen to make sure the backdoor was locked. Then, wanting to recheck the front again, she rushed around the corner and slammed into the large figure looming in the hall.

Kenzie shrieked and threw her fists up.

"Whoa-whoa-whoa-whoa," Ben said. "It's just me. It's okay."

"Jesus! That's twice now!" She sidestepped him and headed for the living room. "And no, it's not okay! There's something out there. It chased me."

Ben peered into the kitchen where he was supposed to be making breakfast. Everything was off and the food was cold. He looked back, ready to feed Kenzie a line, but she'd already disappeared into the foyer.

She stood at the front door and peeled back the curtain, her bulging eyes scanning all directions.

Ben approached carefully to avoid freaking her out a third time. "Kenzie," he said softly. "Hey. What are you talking about? Who's out there?"

"I don't know. I didn't get a good look at it."

"What do you mean? What is it?"

"I don't know! But-but it was tall and skinny."

Tall? Skinny? Ben wracked his brain over the local wildlife fitting that description. "You mean *big*? Like a bear?"

"Is a bear tall and skinny?"

"I don't know. If it's standing upright. And if it's been starving for a while. I guess."

Kenzie gave him a look of ridicule.

"Well, how the hell am I supposed to know what you saw if you don't even know. Whatever it is, it's gone. You're safe."

She exhaled and dropped the curtain. "I know. I know. I'm sorry." She ran her hands through her hair and massaged the sore spot on her scalp. "It must've been some . . . guy. Some local. Some good ol' boy messing with me. I only saw him for a second, but he was like *really* freakin' tall and skinny and wearing all black and shit." She rubbed her eyes and groaned. "All I know is the kids and I are not going out there again until we find out who he—"

Kenzie jumped at the ringing phone. Ben did also.

"Shirley!" she said. "It must be her. She never called last night." Kenzie sped to the desk while Ben pulled back the curtain and took a look outside for himself.

"Hello. Sunrise Bed and Breakfast. Can I help you?"

Kenzie waited for a reply, expecting to hear Shirley's voice. She repeated the greeting.

There was another long moment of silence. Then . . .

"Well hello, Kenzie," the man said on the other line.

Ben watched the blood drain from her face. The phone vibrated in her hand.

"P-P-Paul?"

"Hey, babe." He paused briefly. "Listen closely and don't you even fuckin' think about hanging up. You've been a naughty girl. And I got a question for you, and you better hope for yours and the kids' sake you give me the right goddamn answer."

As he asked Kenzie the question, all ambient noise seemed to suck right out of the room, all except for Paul's voice and the sound of her own thundering heart.

TWENTY

"YOU SURE IT WASN'T HIM fucking with you in the woods? Maybe he's already here and calling from his cell."

"That sure as shit wasn't Paul out there. And he doesn't play games like that. If he was here, he'd be forcing himself inside to . . ." Kenzie pointed to the key on the coffee table. ". . . to get that back."

Scooting to the edge of the couch, Ben leaned forward and stared at what appeared to be a simple house key.

Earlier on the phone, Paul asked Kenzie if she still had the fanny pack. When she said "yes," he told her where a key was hidden in one of its inner pockets. He warned her to keep it safe and that he was on his way to come get it.

After they hung up, she retrieved the key, placed it on the coffee table, and failed to mention anything to Ben about either the stolen money or the pack itself.

"So, how did you get it? And what's it to?"

Kenzie shook her head. "Don't know. I found it in the bottom of one of the boxes I packed," she lied. "Whatever it opens, it's important enough for him to drive all this way to come get."

Ben looked at the key again. It was generic and had no writing or engraving that might provide a clue as to where it came from or what it unlocked.

"Paul has shady friends," Kenzie continued. "People he looks up to. Will do anything for. Maybe he's holding it for them. I don't know."

Ben picked up the key and gave it the once over, wondering if it accessed anything valuable he could use for his daughter. Then he noticed how Kenzie had her arms folded tightly across her stomach, like she was seconds away from vomiting. Seeing her in such extreme distress, he realized now wasn't the time to be angling for some sort of score. Besides, the stupid key could go to anything. He placed it back on the table.

"Can't you just mail it back to him?"

"He said not to do that. That the post office might lose it. So now he's on his way." She exhaled. "God. I do *not* want him here. Maybe I should call the cops and tell them about him coming. Maybe they can stop him."

Ben's leg started to bounce.

"Ya know, mention the past abuse," Kenzie continued. "They can stop him from coming here, right? If I don't want him on the property, that's trespassing, isn't it? There's gotta be something they can do."

Ben shrugged. After a moment, he cleared his throat. "Sure. You *should* call the cops. But, um . . . one thing . . ."

She shook her head slightly, waiting for him to get to the point.

"If you do decide to call, and they tell you they're coming here to talk more about it, can you give me a heads up? You know, because of my lil' beatdown at the bar and all?"

Kenzie sighed and quickly nodded. "Oh, shit. Yeah. I completely forgot. Sure, sure I'll let you know." There was no malice in her inflection. "I'm just—"

"I know. You do what you have to do to protect your family. If that means calling the cops, then do it."

She suddenly recalled the little detail about stealing money from Paul. It was something she'd have to explain to the authorities for them to fully grasp the situation. Even if she did leave it out and he were to show up and get arrested, it would be the first thing he'd fall back on in his defense for being there.

Maybe bringing in the cops wasn't such a good idea. So, Kenzie spun it, "But . . . I don't wanna chase you off."

"Don't worry about me. Okay?"

A long silence crept between them. Kenzie was visibly trembling, staring off into space. Ben could practically see the million thoughts flying around her head, bombarding her brain.

"How long will it take for him to get here?"

Kenzie paced the living room, her arms crossed around her belly, her face taking on an ashen complexion.

"Kenzie?"

She turned to him, almost as if she'd forgotten he was still in the room.

After Ben repeated the question, she answered, "It took us three days, but we started late. Drove three hours the first day, then eight and eight the following days. If he was calling from the apartment, and drives straight through, he could possibly be here tomorrow before dawn."

She groaned and rubbed her aching brow. "He must have somehow remembered this place when I mentioned it once. Never said the name because I didn't know it myself, but I did tell him about a bed and breakfast some relatives owned near Penumbra." She shook her head. "God, how could I have been so stupid?"

The grandfather clock in the hall chimed half past seven.

"Shit," she said. "Breakfast. I gotta get food to everybody upstairs."

"Don't worry about it. It's almost done. We can reheat anything that's cold." Ben figured he was safe. With the one-two punch of the incident in the woods and Paul's surprise call, she'd never think to ask why the food was half-cooked or the stove off. Hell, she was so frazzled, he could tell her anything now and she'd believe it.

And as cruel as it sounded, a part of him realized something like that could be used to his advantage.

~

As Kenzie carried a breakfast tray to the kids' room, the floor creaked behind her. Turning, she suddenly found Myrna in her face, causing her to lurch back.

"Geez! You nearly scared the living shi—"

"Please tell me those aren't for the youngins," Myrna said, staring at the plated omelets. The woman was dressed in her bathrobe and looked like she just rolled out of bed.

"Um . . . yeah. I wanna see if they'll eat a little bit."

"I thought I made it very clear they were only to have broth for now."

"Yeah, but . . ."

Myrna gripped the tray and pulled it close. "Then lemme have this and I'll take it back down to the kitchen."

Kenzie gave some slack but didn't let go. "They need to eat something."

"And they will, but not right now. Their bellies have shrunk and are extremely sensitive. No offense to your great culinary skills, but a greasy, fatty concoction like this will more than likely make them puke or squirt. Maybe both." She motioned to the omelets. "Look. Look at this." Then angled the tray downward.

Grease stretched out of the eggs smothered in cheddar cheese, streaking the white plate with orange oil.

"Well . . . ummm . . ." Kenzie said, nose wrinkling. Maybe Ben had gone a little overboard with the cheese, hoping to entice them.

"As their mother, you really want them eating this shit?"

After a beat, Kenzie yielded and relinquished the tray.

"Now, don't you worry," Myrna continued. "They'll be eating again like lil' piggies soon enough."

Before Kenzie could voice any further objection, Myrna said, "We'll see about getting them a little something later. Maybe saltines. Or some toast. Until then, they should stick only to the broth. Okay?"

Kenzie gave an unsure nod.

"Now you go say good morning to your little ones and I'll take this," she held up the tray, "back downstairs. If this is the same shit we're about to be served, then I'll fix Lucille and I something a little less artery clogging while I'm there." She did an about face and disappeared down the hall.

Kenzie stood there, slightly embarrassed after being scolded by the old woman. "Okay," she mumbled, "whatever." Then she went to wake the kids.

~

"Well, that was fast," Ben said, hearing the approaching footsteps over his shoulder. "Guess they really gobbled it up, huh? Told you the extra cheese would—" He turned, and his proud smile dropped.

Myrna stood at the counter, the food tray hovering a few inches above it. She stared daggers at him with her piercing blue eyes. "*You.* Made. This?"

"Yeah. I . . . ah . . . I'm whipping up some more for you and the other lady upstairs. Should be ready in about—"

Myrna dropped the tray on the counter, where the silver and glassware clanked loudly together. "Don't bother. Cereal will be fine."

Ben scoffed and shook his head while Myrna grabbed a box of shredded wheat from the cabinet to prepare her own breakfast.

~

Kenzie snapped open the curtains and sunlight flooded the room. A collective groan rose behind her.

"Come on, guys. Rise and shine!" She hoped her enthusiasm would not only be believable, but contagious. Tim and Lilly remained cocooned in three-hundred thread count Egyptian cotton.

Kenzie peeled the duvet down to Lilly's shoulders and sat beside her.

When daylight hit the girl's face, she winced and kept her eyes closed. "Bright light! Bright light!" she said in a high-pitched voice, then forcibly giggled and slid up to her mother, nestling her face into the crevice between the mattress and Kenzie's outer thigh.

Kenzie breathed a sigh of relief over the jovial reference to *Gremlins*, one of Lilly's favorite movies. "I take it you're feeling better?" She stroked the girl's hair.

Keeping her face buried, Lilly shrugged then sniffled and coughed into the mattress.

"Hey. You wanna try sitting up for me?"

"Too tired."

"C'mon, baby. Sit up."

"Nooooooo. Sick." Lilly groaned, rolled over, and pulled the covers up to her chin.

Kenzie caressed her daughter's back and stared over at Tim on the opposite bed. The comforter was pulled over his head with only the tip of his nose and chin peeking out. He also let out a phlegmy cough. "Hey, Maaa," he said, the greeting coming out as more of a croak.

"Morning, baby. How about you? Feeling better?"

"Uh-huh." Then he turned away and fell silent.

Kenzie's eyes shifted to the two empty coffee mugs on the nightstand. She looked back at her children and quietly sighed.

~

While Kenzie was still upstairs with the kids, Ben was behind closed doors, packing the last of his items into the duffle bag. He had to be ready to leave at a moment's notice in case Kenzie changed her mind about calling the cops. Although he really liked her and wished her and the kids no harm, it was becoming far too risky for him to stay much longer. Until then, if that shitbag Paul arrived before he left, he'd gladly give the guy a long overdue ass kicking. He might have made up the whole story about defending some girl at the bar to win over Kenzie's trust, but beating on a woman—or especially a child— was something Ben would not tolerate. His daughter Evie was close to Tim's age and the thought of anyone putting her in harm's way made his blood boil. In fact, it was the very reason for his own cross-country trek, to get Evie away from her junkie mother.

If Paul were to show his face around there, Ben would have to slam it through a wall. For Kenzie. And especially for the kids. Of course, doing so would cause him unwanted attention. And given his criminal record and the stolen goods in his possession, any cop running his ID would see his parole violation and toss his ass back in jail.

Then where would Evie be?

Ben sat on the edge of the mattress and lowered his head. He honestly couldn't give a rat's ass about the two old hermits upstairs. If Paul arrived and started trouble, they were in no danger unless they stepped in to try to stop things, which he thought was highly unlikely. The women would probably remain locked in their bedrooms until the screaming stopped downstairs.

Could he abandon Kenzie and the kids like that?

Come on, now. You don't even know if this guy is even coming. Besides, you don't owe anybody shit except for Evie. Staying here is gonna put you smack dab in the middle of a shitstorm you have no business being in.

Still, he couldn't skip out on them when their version of the big, bad wolf might soon arrive on their doorstep. He stared down at his duffle bag and quickly came up with a compromise.

The .38 snub-nose inside. He could leave her the stolen pistol and a box of ammo, which was the next best thing to stopping Paul himself. Before making his exit, he'd wipe his prints off the gun and place a note on the dresser telling her where it was. That is, after he checked out the two rooms on the third floor.

There was no way in hell he planned to leave the house without doing so first.

～

Although concerned about the kids' slow recovery, Kenzie was slightly relieved they weren't up and about to see how much of a nervous wreck she was over Paul's impending visit. If asked, she'd inform them only to keep them vigilant, but for now they would remain in the dark until some plan of action was decided.

Standing at the living room window, she pulled back the curtain and stared at the driveway. Whoever chased her earlier—scaring her half to death—hopefully had their fun and moved on, making way for a different type of sicko to arrive.

What was Paul going to do when he showed up? One thing was certain, he wouldn't just take the key and leave quietly. Oh, no. There'd be some sort of repercussion for her betrayal and theft, then a second round of punishment when she'd be unable to pay back his money immediately. Even if she gathered all the cash in the safe, it wouldn't equal half of what she owed him. Besides, that money was reserved for running the inn, since she didn't know how long Shirley would be gone.

But, what if . . .

What if Ben acted as some sort of go-between? He could hand over the key and tell Paul to piss off because the money was already spent.

Paul liked to act like a real Tommy Tough Nuts with his women, but he would probably be a complete coward when confronted by another guy, especially someone bigger and who was threatening to beat his ass. Kenzie grinned. *How sweet it'd be if it would work out that way, huh?* Of course, for any of this to happen she'd have to come clean to Ben about stealing the money. Surely, he'd understand her motives given the circumstances. Then again . . .

Okay. Stop it. One thing at a time.

Her eyes shifted from the driveway over to her Jeep parked in the side lot. It'd be best to move it around back and out of sight. To leave it exposed was like having a blinking neon sign advertising, VEHICLE TO VANDALIZE! STEP RIGHT UP! Without a doubt, Paul would smash her windows and puncture the tires in order to call it even on what he was owed, especially once he found out his money was gone.

Her SUV was one thing, but hopefully he wouldn't do anything *really* stupid, like something to the house. When inviting Kenzie to stay, Shirley already mentioned they weren't looking for trouble. And now that she was gone . . .

Which reminded Kenzie . . .

She went to the counter and checked the phone for a dial tone. It came in loud and clear, letting her know there wasn't a problem on her end. So why hadn't Shirley called?

What if she was in an accident?

Wait! The piece of paper with Nina's number taped to the fridge.

With so much going on, she forgot all about it.

After a quick trip to the kitchen, Kenzie returned with the number and dialed it. While the line rang, her free hand tapped the counter with woodpecker-like speed.

There was a click and a moment of silence.

"You've reached a number that has been disconnected or no longer in service," a recording said on the other end.

Her pulse quickened. "Okay. You dialed wrong. That's all." Reciting the numbers aloud, she carefully punched each one again.

"You've reached a number that has been disconnected or—"

Kenzie slammed the phone onto the cradle and stepped back, her hands raised in the air. "All right. This is bullshit." She snatched the number and ran back to the kitchen.

Shirley's notebook of instructions still sat on the counter, open to the last page with Nina's number written in red across the top. After a quick comparison, Kenzie's heart sunk. The numbers were identical. And utterly freaking useless.

Either Shirley had mistakenly jotted down the wrong number, *twice,* or this Nina lady forgot to pay her damn phone bill. Kenzie shut the notebook and pushed it away. *One thing at a time,* she told herself again, the phrase now becoming her new mantra.

Knowing it was best to focus on things within her control, she strode down the hall to fetch her keys and move the Jeep around back.

~

Ben heard the passing footsteps outside his door, then turned back to the dresser and finished writing his note to Kenzie. It read:

Sorry I can't stay. Had to move on. Left you something to use on Paul as a last resort. My closet, top shelf. Be careful, it's loaded. If it comes down to it, just point it at his chest and squeeze the trigger. He deserves nothing better.

The .38 snub-nose revolver sat exposed within his unzipped bag. Ben didn't know if Kenzie had ever shot a gun before, but his instructions were simple enough.

The note was harsh. But to the point.

He slowly nodded and thought, *And given the circumstance, the best I can do.*

~

A chill rippled through Kenzie on her way to the Jeep. After the incident jogging this morning, her vehicle seemed to be parked far too close to the woods now. She scanned the trees and picked up her pace, pressing the key fob numerous times to make sure the doors would open. Once locked safely inside, she gripped the steering wheel tight and turned the ignition key.

Her heart skipped a beat when nothing happened.

Okay. You didn't turn it all the way. That's all. She flipped the key back, then forward as far as it would go.

The engine not only wouldn't fire up, it didn't even click. She tried again and again to the same results.

"Fuck! Fuck-fuck-fuck! Fuuuck!!" Pounding the steering wheel, she continued screaming as the sealed windows censored her obscenities.

TWENTY-ONE

"PLEASE TELL ME YOU KNOW something about cars."

Ben stared at Kenzie, who stood in his doorway and looked one step away from having a nervous breakdown.

Seconds earlier, he was about to wipe the revolver clean of any fingerprints and put it in the closet when she knocked on his door. Instead, the pistol went back in his bag, which was pushed under the bed, out of sight.

"Well . . . what's it doing?"

"Nothing. It won't start."

He rubbed the back of his neck. "Okay. I'll take a look at it, but I can't promise you anything."

~

After a minute of poking and prodding under the hood, it became clear Ben knew very little about cars. He made sure the battery was connected and checked for any loose wires or broken belts. Or as he put it, for "anything hanging down." After that, he meekly shrugged and suggested maybe Myrna could help.

Kenzie scoffed.

"I know. But what have you got to lose?"

Moments later, Kenzie stood in front of the old woman's door, summoning the courage to knock.

She knew, without a vehicle, they'd be in deep trouble if one of the kids suddenly took a turn for the worse. Or if Paul showed up and got violent. Hopefully, having Ben around would prevent something like that from happening.

Although she would love to see Paul get his face punched in, after giving it more thought, it wasn't fair to get Ben involved in her mess. Her solution was to place the key in an envelope and leave it in the mailbox at the end of the driveway, far away from the house. She'd call Paul on his cell, tell him where the key was, and promise to repay the money, mailing him a cashier's check once able to recoup the finances. Then everyone would remain behind locked doors until Kenzie felt confident that he moved on. Hopefully, he'd leave without incident.

Yeah, right.

But first things first. She needed a working vehicle as insurance to avoid being trapped if things went south.

Kenzie took a deep breath and rapped on Myrna's door. She stared at her feet, then up and down the hall, debating how long to wait before knocking again. Maybe the woman was next door.

She gulped. *Oh, God. Lucille's room.*

Was she prepared to knock on *that* door looking for Myrna? And what if she did and Myrna wasn't there, but instead Lucille called out for her to enter? Was she ready for that?

Hell, no! I'll act like I didn't hear her and tear ass out of—

Kenzie recoiled when Myrna's door opened wide enough for the woman to stick her head out. "Yes?" Her inflection reeked of annoyance.

Kenzie smiled. "Hi. Sorry to disturb you. I know this is gonna sound weird, but by some off chance, do you know anything about cars?"

~

"Back in the day, my husband, Charlie, used to own a rinky-dink repair shop."

The two women walked down the front porch steps and made their way to the Jeep.

"I used to give him a hand on occasion," Myrna continued, "after his mechanics went home for the day. I'd study there after hours while working on my nursing degree." She grunted. "Christ, my textbooks were always covered in greasy little fingerprints from poking around that shithole all night." She paused then snickered and gave

Kenzie a nudge. "Bahhh, that sounded kinda dirty, didn't it?"

Kenzie shrugged and smiled in disbelief that Myrna actually had a sense of humor. And a dirty one at that.

"Whenever I'd pull my nose outta the books long enough to hand Charlie tools, I'd watch what he was doing. In a way, our jobs were quite similar: diagnosing a problem from the inner workings of things, whether it's man or machine. You see, his patients leaked oil, antifreeze, brake and transmission fluid. Mine? Blood, puke, shit, and piss." She backhanded Kenzie's shoulder. "Am I right?"

Kenzie flinched. "Yeah. Never looked at it that way."

A long silence accompanied them on the way to the vehicle. Kenzie's mind reeled over the revelation about the woman. Who knew she was married? And hadn't Myrna been living there with Lucille for something like thirty years? "Charlie, huh? So, where's Charlie now?"

"Gone. Just disappeared one day."

"He left?"

"Yeah, but apparently not by his own volition. Unless he was in such a hurry he forgot to take his left arm."

A mix of confusion and repulsion clouded Kenzie's face.

"Yep. We only found his left arm that morning. That and about five pints of blood all over the garage. Probably died of hypervolemic shock. You know, bled out for those that don't speak Greek."

Kenzie slowed to a stop. "God. What happened?"

Myrna paused. "Don't know exactly. But do know he racked up a lot of gambling debts. Cops thought it was more of a robbery gone bad. I called bullshit on that since all the cash was still left in the register. Anyhoo, he was working late at the shop to finish up a brake job. I'd gone to bed, and never knew he didn't come home until after the police called at the ass crack of dawn. His day-shift manager discovered the scene. And like I said, that register was still full, so they weren't after any cash. Or, I guess, his left arm for that matter."

Kenzie couldn't believe the woman would make such a joke. Myrna read the look on her face.

"This was over forty-years ago, hon. I buried that shit, along with his left arm, a long time ago. I admit, I was lost without him, but I eventually moved on with the help of some friends. Hell, even had a fling with a nice fellow for a while." She smiled and shook her head. "Oh, Roman. He was a real charmer, that one. Sure had a way with the ladies. Anyway, it was Lucille and the others who taught me how to stand on my own two feet again."

"I didn't know you and Lucille knew each other before you became her nurse."

Myrna suddenly glared at her. It was like a wolf eyeing a lamb, and Kenzie had no idea why her innocent remark drew such a response.

Distant thunder rumbled. A dark band of clouds along the horizon were approaching.

Myrna blinked and smiled. "Storm's a comin'," she said, then playfully smacked Kenzie's shoulder again. "Come on. Let's give her a look before it hits."

~

Ben spied the two women walking out the front door and down the porch steps toward the SUV. He was genuinely concerned about Kenzie's sudden lack of transportation. Although his suggestion about asking Myrna for help wasn't a ploy to get them out of the house, the result turned out to be truly serendipitous. He rushed into Kenzie's room and snatched the keyring from the closet.

After a quick glimpse outside to confirm the coast was still clear, he slid behind the counter and unlocked the wall-mounted lock box. Out of the two keys needed, only the one for 3A was inside. It would have to be good enough for now.

He removed the key to Myrna's room and relocked the box, then went back to the window and saw Kenzie and Myrna stopped on the front lawn.

Oh, shit. He ducked down.

Had they seen him through the sheer curtains?

Before aborting his mission, he peeked out again and saw them facing *away* from the house. He watched for a few moments and it appeared whatever they were discussing had nothing to do about him. Still, Ben knew it was best to return the key ring before heading upstairs, in case their conversation was about fetching tools for the car that were locked away somewhere.

Once the women continued away from the house, Ben rushed back to Kenzie's room and returned her keys.

~

"Hop in and give it a try, so I can see what she's doing. Or not doing."

Kenzie did as she was told, and the engine remained silent.

Myrna pulled her head out from under the hood. "Are you even turning the key?"

Kenzie did it again. "Yes. It's not doing anything." She repeated the action a third time. "See?"

"All right. All right. Give it a break."

Kenzie hopped out and met Myrna, who wiggled the battery connections. "Probably the alternator. As for the battery, nothing's loose, but . . ." she pointed to the white, flakey crust coating its terminals. "See this shit here? It's dried acid. Might be interfering with the connection."

Kenzie gave an "oooooh-yeeeeah" face, as if she knew what the lady was talking about.

"Probably won't do jack, but let's wash it off anyway to rule it out."

"Okay. But I don't think the garden hose is long enough to reach—"

"Get outta here. We only need two large cups of water with a little baking soda mixed in one."

~

Cloaked in the hallway shadows, Ben peeled back a curtain at one of the third-floor windows and peered down at the Jeep, where Myrna was pointing something out to Kenzie under the hood.

He chuckled in disbelief. *Guess this Myrna chick really does know something about cars!*

After a final check to make sure the hall was empty and Lucille's door was closed, Ben crept forward, stuck the key in 3A's latch, and gave it a turn. The lock flipped over with a loud, metallic clack. He winced and checked his surroundings again, then twisted the metal knob, opening the door enough for a peek inside.

Myrna's room was dark. The drawn, heavy curtains blocked all sunlight except at the edges, where a few inches of light spread across the wall, giving off an almost ethereal glow.

Before entering, Ben verified the bed was empty. He was told Lucille was bedridden but wanted to make sure it meant confined to her *own* bed, not moving between rooms for a change of scenery.

He stepped inside, closed the door, and clicked on a nearby floor lamp. Its low-watt bulb failed to properly light the room, but at least revealed what he'd be dealing with.

It was all standard furnishing. A queen bed sat along the far wall. A mirror mounted to a triple dresser reflected a large oak desk across the room. The desk was buried under piles of paperwork, books, and various clutter. A medium-sized refrigerator sat beside it and, next to that, a small microwave and sink. There were two other doors, most likely to the bathroom and closet.

The room reminded him of his first apartment, an efficiency. Once considered claustrophobic, it later seemed like the Taj Mahal when compared to the prison cell he occupied for the past two years.

Knowing the clock was ticking, he sprang into action, checking the dresser and snagging a few rings, necklaces, and diamond earrings that hopefully weren't costume jewelry. He shoved them deep in his pocket and moved over to the desk, finding both drawers only full of junk.

Numerous apothecary mortars and pestles lined the desktop, a fine layer of powder coating each bowl. Bags of dried herbs and other plants sat among the mishmash. Ben sniffed a few. He snorted at their pungent odor and tossed the bags back onto the desk.

A check of the refrigerator's contents found the expected items: food, drink, and condiments, along with a small tray of medicine. The labels on the tiny vials might as well have been in Latin. Since he was neither druggie nor dealer, Ben had no interest in them. A coffee can on the counter contained only aromatic grinds.

There was nothing between the mattress and box spring or under the bed. The bathroom medicine cabinet was also void of any valuables.

While checking inside the toilet tank, a loud thump made Ben flinch and almost drop the porcelain lid. Thinking Myrna had returned to her room, his heart pounded against his ribcage. He quickly, yet quietly, replaced the lid and stepped into the tub, ducking behind the opaque floral curtain.

There was silence. Then scratching.

Ben cocked his head to the side.

Where the hell was it coming from? Not from the bedroom . . . but behind the wall next to him.

From inside the closet.

He placed a hot ear against the cold tile and listened.

Another thump, only lighter. Then the scratching faded, as if moving away.

It was probably some varmint—a raccoon or possum—that found its way inside and was now traveling between the walls. In any case, it wasn't Myrna but a damn good reminder to get his ass in gear, finish searching the room, and get the hell out of there.

Opening the closet, he flipped on the light inside, and his eyes widened. Void of wardrobe, the walls of the small room were lined with shallow shelves from floor to ceiling. Some were stocked two layers deep with jars of powder, dried plants, and various knick-knacks such as soiled paint brushes, half-melted candles, and small animal bones. Other shelves contained rows of old books.

Ironically, with the walls being so cluttered, the floor contained only a thick carpet mat, positioned dead center of the closet. Ben stepped into the shallow space and eyed the book spines for any familiar titles or authors. He'd seen various episodes of that pawn shop show where they appraised some rare book for tens of thousands of dollars. Most were first editions of a literary classic like *Dracula* or *Moby Dick*, but there was one episode where someone brought in an early Stephen King autographed novel, which sold for five grand. Adding something like that to his duffle bag would be worth the extra weight, especially if it fetched such a pretty penny on the secondhand market.

Unfortunately, none of the books had dust jackets, and the dim lighting above from the forty-watt bulb made it hard to read any printing on their spines. He leaned in, his eyes narrowed. Some had markings like Roman numerals but nothing forming words. A few books peppered throughout the library appeared to be leatherbound. Those had to be worth something. Ben selected one and searched for a title page. It was blank. Flipping deeper inside, its contents were entirely handwritten like a journal. It wasn't in English either. And numerous pages contained odd diagrams and sketches.

Ben tossed it aside and grabbed another leatherbound. It too was handwritten in a foreign language and contained various drawings. Thumbing further through it, he stopped at a few of the illustrations to see if he could figure out what the book was about. One crude sketch showed two figures lying next to each other as if asleep. There were squiggly lines above each, like heat waves rising off their bodies. Above the waves were arrows going back and forth to the figures. He flipped to the next drawing and saw a series of symbols forming a circle and, at its center, a crudely drawn house. Ben squinted and angled the book toward the light.

He recognized one of the symbols. It looked a hell of a lot like the carving on the tree outside. The one with the eye bleeding tears of sap.

A muffled thud, vibrating the floorboards underfoot, snapped his attention out of the book. Although he was pretty sure it came from the next room, it could've easily been the front door opening and closing downstairs.

Ben quickly replaced the book in the open slot and exited the closet. Shutting off the floor lamp, he ducked out of the bedroom and slid up to the hall window to confirm if the noise heard earlier had been Kenzie or Myrna entering the house.

To his surprise, the two women were still at the SUV. Which meant the sound came from . . .

He turned and had to look twice at Lucille's door before accepting it was ajar. It was only an inch-wide gap, but that sucker was definitely open now.

Okay. This ain't right.

He licked his lips. His pulse pounded from the adrenaline rush. He'd already come this far.

Fuck it. At least take a peek.

Ben slowly pushed open the door an additional inch or so. Two small lamps, draped in sheer red fabric, cast a crimson glow over the murky room. While his eyes adjusted to the odd lighting, sickly breathing rose out of the gloom.

He paused, then poked his head in a little further to investigate.

A king bed sat at the center of the room, cloaked in a flowing canopy with an eerie glow emanating from within. Projected across its fabric screen was the silhouette of an open-mouthed figure lying face up.

Ben froze and studied Lucille's shadow. Her nasty, gelatinous wheezing—which he assumed was snoring—grew louder.

Don't wake her and this'll be a piece of cake.

With his eyes already adjusting to the dim setting, he saw the jewelry box on the dresser. Its lid was up, exposing something shiny. Golden.

He pushed open the door and stepped inside. Huge mounds of clothing were spread across the room, some piled waist high and concealing an entire corner. A large wicker basket, footlocker trunk, and recliner sat half buried by the garments.

As the cadence of heavy breathing continued, Ben silently closed the door behind him. The woman's silhouette remained frozen, her mouth still open.

He carefully maneuvered the clothes piles to reach the jewelry box, then plucked out various diamond and gold pieces, shoving them in his pocket where they lightly clinked against his Zippo. So far, the score was good, but what he needed was cash—not only was it more convenient, it avoided the high risk that came with selling stolen goods on the secondhand market.

He rummaged through the dresser drawers and, when finding nothing, continued to the wicker basket. Expecting it to be full of blankets or clothing, it was empty except for a strong, musky odor like that of a wet dog. The footlocker beside it had nothing of value inside either.

Using his foot, he stirred a few of the piles of clothing to make sure they weren't concealing anything valuable, then opened the closet door and was greeted by utter blackness and a blast of cold air.

When a light switch couldn't be found on either wall, inside or out, he slowly extended his hand until it disappeared at the elbow. He waved back and forth, waiting to feel a string suspended from an overhead bulb. An insane scenario suddenly flashed in his mind, causing a fresh chill to lift his balls up into his body: what if some*thing* licked his outstretched fingers? Or he stuck them into a gaping mouth waiting to snap shut like an ivory bear trap?

With the awful wheezing continuing behind him, his extreme case of the creeps won out over rationality, and he quickly withdrew his hand. He felt for the Zippo in his pocket. Because the sound of its strike or light from its flame might give him away, it'd be best to step inside and close the door behind him before firing it up (hoping, of course, the small space wasn't stockpiled with open jerrycans of gasoline).

He checked the bed to confirm the old woman hadn't moved, then entered the closet.

As the door began to shut, the floor shifted and dropped about a half inch, snapping loudly. He froze, terrified the floor was about to give out.

Waiting a few moments for his heart to start beating again, Ben peeked out to make sure the noise hadn't woken the crone. Her silhouette remained the same and, more importantly, her rhythmic snoring hadn't faltered. He sighed in relief and bounced ever-so-slightly to test the stability of the floorboards.

Resuming control of the situation, Ben sealed himself inside and struck the zippo. He found himself standing on a patch of square carpet with only about three inches of the wood floor surrounding it. His attention shifted to the shelving stockpiled with items even odder than what was found in Myrna's closet. Rows of pickling jars contained fleshy oddities and vegetation suspended in golden liquid. The wall behind him, meant for hanging clothes, only sported an empty rod. No surprise there, since it seemed the woman's entire wardrobe littered the floor outside.

He went for a closer look at a jar of baby pickled something-or-other when the floor popped again. He started upright, then froze for a few seconds. While leaning over to look at his feet, the wood beneath him groaned. Something very odd was happening down there.

Ben squatted to pull back the carpet and view the actual floorboards. Surprisingly, the mat wouldn't move. It seemed to be glued down. He felt under the edge bordering the back wall, and his fingertip stopped on something metal and raised.

Okay. Now we're talking.

He ran his finger farther down until finding the second hinge. His pulse quickened at the realization he was standing on top of a trapdoor. It had to be some sort of hidden compartment where the cash was kept.

Ben pinched the shag carpet and tried to raise the lid, but the space within the closet was too tight. Even straddling the hatch, his feet covered its seam, his body weight pinning it closed. He shifted and repositioned himself in the cramped area but clumsily backed into a shelf, causing the jars to loudly clank. Frustrated, he rose to reassess the situation.

Because of the limited floor space, the only way to raise the lid would be to step out of the closet and lean back in. He snapped the zippo closed and stood in the darkness to clear his racing mind. Then it dawned on him. There had been an identical rug in Myrna's closet. He'd have to backtrack to her room and check. But first . . .

Ben slowly opened the door and was immediately hit by the old woman's wet, labored snoring, which now rivaled the sound of fingernails raking a chalkboard.

Padding out of the closet, he turned and dropped to his knees, then leaned into the shallow space and reached for the carpet. After silently counting to three, he lifted the hatch. Its hinges creaked like those on a decrepit coffin. A puff of air blew out of the opening, carrying with it the pungent, wet dog smell from earlier. Only this time it was stronger. Much stronger.

To mask his Zippo strike, he timed it with Lucille's sharp, raspy inhale, then lowered the flame into the opening. The actual compartment was only about two and a half feet wide by two feet deep, its interior all scratched to hell. While the immediate space was empty, it stretched much farther back than anticipated, tunneling underneath the wall until a sheet of darkness pushed back against the Zippo's light.

Ben rose and braced himself on the edge of the opening. *What the hell is this?* he thought. The whole thing appeared more like an air shaft. Or a crawlspace. Nothing was stored inside unless it was pushed all the way down to remain out of sight. If that were the case (and it very well may be, considering all the scratch marks) there had to be a rope used to pull the item back for access. He felt around for something.

While still on his knees and debating his next move, he heard faint scratching from somewhere down the shaft. Ben aimed an ear into the passageway.

It must've been the animal heard earlier while in Myrna's bathroom. It was looping back, getting closer.

His arms sprung erect, pushing his face away from the hole. The last thing he needed was a run-in with a rabid raccoon. That would kind of throw a wrench into his whole . . . plan . . . of . . .

His thought died over a terrifying realization.

Ben cocked his head at the sudden silence while staring down at the Zippo's flame.

Lucille's snoring . . . had stopped.

Hunched on all fours in the closet doorway, the hair prickled along his scalp as if a spider's egg sack ruptured over his head. His mouth went dry, heart strained a faster beat, and eyes ticked back and forth.

Yet, he refused to turn and look behind him.

His fingers were frozen, unable to even snap the Zippo closed to extinguish the flame giving him away.

It didn't matter anymore. It was too late. He knew he was being watched.

The icy chill racing up his spine exploded like a roman candle against the base of his skull, finally breaking his paralysis. His head pivoted until he saw the crooked shadow of the woman sitting up on the bed, her head aimed in his direction.

A milky cataract eye stared out from between the canopy's seam, locking on him with a Gorgon-like glare.

The woman spasmed silently for what felt like an eternity, until a hideous cackle erupted out of her throat. The terrifying sound shot across the room and clamped over Ben's skull, clawing deep into his ears, burrowing into his brain.

No. The clawing he heard wasn't inside his head, but back in the closet. Directly below him. Inside the shaft.

Ben whirled around. The Zippo's flame illuminated a demonic face staring up at him from out of the opening. Its hellfire eyes widened, and a mouthful of ivory fangs snapped open.

Before he could scream, two arms sprung out of the passageway and wrapped around his waist like a pair of ebony boa constrictors. Ben dropped the Zippo and braced himself with both hands to prevent being pulled into the hole. As he fought to push up and away, the creature violently yanked down, it's inhuman strength easily overpowering him.

Ben collapsed flat to the floor, his head raking the underside of the raised trapdoor on his way down.

The blow stunned him. His hips sunk deeper into the opening, leaving his soft belly vulnerable for disembowelment from below. Before it could happen, he panicked and clawed at the wall in a futile attempt to pull himself back up. His fingernails raked, bent, and snapped off, leaving bloody tips. His legs kicked out. He tried rising to his knees to regain some sort of leverage.

But his attacker's long, muscular arms readjusted, wrapping tighter around Ben's waist, pulling his body downward until finally straining his spine to its breaking point.

Ben opened his mouth to scream his daughter's name—the first and only word his fevered brain could formulate—but the creature wrenched down and broke his spine with a loud, sickening crack.

The air exploded from Ben's lungs in a pink mist, bloodying the wall. His arms and legs floundered as if lit up by a thousand volts of electricity. The thing pushed his body up and instantly heaved it back down, splintering another section of his spinal column. It repeated the action again and again like a dog ripping away a chew toy from its owner's grasp—providing a little slack, then fiercely yanking back.

It shattered his vertebrae until Ben gruesomely folded backwards and sunk into the hole as a suit of broken bones. His calves flung up and hooked over his shoulders, heels slamming into his chest, then his body was sucked deeper into the crawlspace. The violent action rippled the floorboards, causing the trap door to bounce and drop shut, sealing all evidence of the assault, except for the blood spray on the wall.

After a long moment of silence, the ghastly, unblinking eye peering out from behind the canopy pulled back. The thin, crooked shadow slowly lowered flat to the mattress. Then the gargled breathing resumed, only this time softer, more relaxed.

Satisfied.

TWENTY-TWO

AS THE MIXTURE OF BAKING-SODA and warm water neutralized the acid, the battery terminals bubbled like a witch's caldron.

Myrna rubbed her fingers together furiously. Kenzie first thought she might have been burned by acid but quickly realized the old woman never touched the battery, only dumped the water solution over it. She was just doing her weird-ass, nervous tick.

Once the bubbling ceased, Myrna pointed at the large cup of distilled water in Kenzie's hand. "Okay. Pour that on and rinse that shit off the battery."

Kenzie hesitated. "Pour it on? That's not gonna short out anything?"

Myrna gave her a look as if she just found Kenzie eating dirt. "Oh, come on, now. You watched me pour water all over the damn thing a second ago. Did anything bad happen then?"

"Well, no. But yours had baking soda in it so I thought . . ." Kenzie deflated. "Never mind. I told you I don't know jack about cars."

"Would you just pour it over?!"

Kenzie did as commanded and washed off the mixture.

After Myrna wiped the battery dry with a clean rag, she said, "Okay. Try starting her."

Kenzie flipped the key. The engine remained stubborn and silent.

Myrna shrugged, slammed the hood shut, and wiped her hands with the rag. Kenzie climbed out from behind the wheel, clinging to the false hope the old woman still had something up her sleeve.

"Put a bullet in her head," Myrna said. "The old girl's toast. Probably the alternator. You'll need to have her towed into town and looked at."

Kenzie slumped on the hood and groaned. She sure as shit didn't have the money for something like that.

Distant thunder rumbled, mocking Kenzie's hopelessness. Both women turned and stared at the darkening sky above the treetops.

"Aaaaand . . . so it begins." Myrna said. Without another word, she turned and headed back to the house.

Kenzie rolled her eyes. The woman had a real knack for being so goddamn weird.

~

By the time Kenzie had the Jeep locked up tight, Myrna already retired to her room.

Once inside, Kenzie flipped the deadbolts on the front door and stood alone in the lobby, leaning on the check-in counter while nervously drumming her fingers across its surface. The house was quiet. Too quiet.

It made her extremely uneasy.

Needing a comforting face, she rapped on Ben's door. He should be kept abreast of the situation, since she couldn't give him a ride as originally offered. If wanting to leave anytime soon, he'd better do so before the storm hit.

She knocked again, harder, took a step back, and waited. Glancing up and down the hallway, her mind drifted back to the Jeep. Maybe they could push it behind the house to keep it out of sight. Or maybe . . . maybe if the ground sloped enough to the backyard, she could put it in neutral and, with a little help from gravity and inertia, just take care of the whole thing herself.

Putting Ben on hold for now, Kenzie walked to the kitchen to check the backyard and see if there was a clear path for the vehicle to travel.

~

Once Kenzie's footsteps faded down the hall, Ben's partially unzipped bag (the exposed .38 pistol on top) was pulled deeper into the closet by its shoulder strap, now stretched tight and disappearing into the crawlspace. The bag teetered on the edge of the opening then, with a heavy thud, dropped inside and out of sight.

In the bedroom proper, all evidence of Ben's stay had been erased. All except for an overlooked item: the upside-down sheet of paper on the dresser, the note to Kenzie about where to find the gun for protection.

The closet door creaked shut and was followed by the muffled thump of the trap door falling back into place.

~

Stepping onto the back porch to scout for someplace to conceal the Jeep, Kenzie was greeted by laundry flapping in the backyard. Temporarily abandoning her plans, she quickly plucked the clothes off the line and tossed them into a basket. Then something in the dirt caught her eye.

Footprints.

She paused and cocked her head. Bare feet? *Large* bare feet. They came from the side of the house, then to the woods, and back again, branching out in various directions, but always funneling to the same spot around the corner.

Kenzie followed the tracks, which eventually stopped at the wooden lattice on the far side of the back porch. She stared past the grid and saw a murky crawlspace under the platform.

Looking closer at the dirt, she noticed it also contained handprints—large ones, calloused and cracked, with fingers eerily double the length of what was natural.

The skin prickled along her nape at the oddity.

It's just distorted, she thought. *Only looks that way 'cause they slid their hand forward after planting it in the dirt.* Or so she told herself.

A few of the prints had the heel of the palm flush with the lattice, the spindly fingers pointing out at the yard. Given their position, either someone was doing a handstand against the wall or . . .

They had been crawling in and out from under the porch.

Kenzie spun and scanned the tree line. *The creep from the woods!*

She shuddered and looked closer at the lattice, now noticing it was only propped up against the porch, not fastened to it. She scurried back to a safer distance and spotted a bow rake next to a planter erupting in weeds. Using it to knock the lattice away, she aimed the garden tool at the opening, ready to strike anything that might jump out.

Nearly a minute passed before she gathered the courage to inch closer and stare inside. With the cover off, more sunlight made its way in, but it only extended so far.

The murkier area deeper under the porch piqued both her curiosity and suspicion.

After retrieving a flashlight, Kenzie waved its beam back and forth, searching for anything odd that might warrant a call to the authorities or, to a lesser extent, animal control. Throughout the cramped space, wispy cobwebs snared pieces of brittle leaves, dead insects, and other debris, all except for a cleared path continuing beyond the porch and under the house. Somebody had been under there.

Who the hell was snooping around their property, crawling under the inn? Maybe local kids goofing around. Or maybe the gas man or an exterminator that Shirley hired to check under the place before their arrival.

Highly unlikely, but it would make sleeping at night a little easier if she fooled herself into thinking such. Because the last thing she wanted to imagine was a hole in the house where some sort of animal—or God forbid, a person—could enter and wreak havoc in the dead of night.

~

After gathering the remaining clothes off the line, Kenzie tried Ben's door again. She could really use a second opinion on the porch situation. A fresh set of eyes. "Ben! You in there?"

Still no response.

Okay, if the guy's taking a shower or a crap, he's had plenty of time to wrap things up. She knocked again. Harder. And waited. Then found herself reaching for the handle. *Whoa, hold up. So much for privacy around here, huh?*

But what if he was hurt in there? Slipped and fell? Or God forbid, had a heart attack or stroke and that's why he wasn't answering. She continued lying to herself that, in the interest of Ben's welfare, the best thing to do was to enter. She turned the knob, found the door unlocked, and opened it a few inches.

"Ben? It's me, Kenzie. You okay? You decent?"

Silence.

"Hey. I'm coming in."

Her heart sunk finding the room empty of his belongings. She went to the closet and found it barren.

He was gone.

Kenzie's emotions ricocheted from one to the other.

Confusion. *Why leave without saying goodbye? I thought he decided to stay.*

Hurt. *I thought he was my friend.*

Anger. *Goddammit. I actually thought he was decent.*

She scoffed at her own naivety. *You are so blind when it comes to men.*

Then she noticed a sheet of paper on the dresser with ink faintly bleeding through and a pen resting on top. She flipped it over and saw his note.

"Present to use on Paul . . ."

After reading it, she went to the closet as instructed and stepped inside. The floorboards under the shag mat buckled slightly, then snapped. She stared down at her feet, unaware of the trapdoor underneath, thinking it was only a soft spot of wood in the old house. She looked back at the top shelf. From his note, it was obvious he'd left her a gun . . . and thankfully had the foresight and consideration to keep it out of the kids' reach.

Although he flat out abandoned her at the worst possible time, at least the guy left something she could actually use.

She debated the line she was about to cross by accepting the gun. If Paul became violent, would she have the guts to pull it on him? And, more importantly, if things escalated, could she pull the trigger and shoot him?

If she choked, he could take it away and use it against her.

Her thoughts turned to her children. To their safety. And how Paul was probably coward enough to lash out at them to get to her.

Could I kill him if he was about to hurt my kids? she asked herself.

You're goddamn right I could. She reached up and ran a hand across the top shelf for the gun. Rising on her tippy toes, she stretched a little farther until her fingertips scraped the back wall. So . . . where was it?

She grabbed a chair and stood on it, putting her head and shoulders above the shelf.

There was no gun. Was all this some sort of sick joke?

Heat flushed her chest. She wanted to give Ben a piece of her mind, call him a coward, and ask him why? He couldn't be that far down the driveway.

She hopped off the chair and marched to the bedroom exit, ready to give chase even as the threatening storm clouds approached.

Then she paused. Took a breath. Shook her head.

This is your *fight. For* your *family. Don't get distracted. So.* Fuck. *Him.*

"Now get your shit together and figure something out."

~

Hours before nightfall, the dark clouds rolled in and opened up, dumping thick sheets of rain across the area. The woods were only a few yards away, yet barely visible through the gray haze. Staring out at the storm, Kenzie stood on the front porch and held an envelope with Paul's name on it. It contained not only the mysterious key he was coming all this way for, but a short note apologizing for stealing his money and a promise to mail it back once she recouped the amount.

It wasn't clear when he'd arrive, but she wanted to have everything ready in case his call earlier had been from the road (although he probably wouldn't have left home without first confirming where she was, and if she still had the key). Whatever the case, he was coming and that was that.

The original plan of running the key out to the mailbox by the main road vanished after her Jeep failed to start, and later when it started raining like hell.

Instead, Kenzie taped the envelope to the glass on the front door, so it would be impossible to miss. She also looped the strap of the fanny pack around the doorknob and left it hanging there in case it contained any more surprises.

Just take the whole damn thing and go, she thought. *Don't give him another reason to come back.*

The inn would remain locked down until long after the envelope was gone. If the key was all he wanted, there was no need to talk. Of course, the stolen money complicated things, but maybe he'd dismiss the nominal amount when compared to whatever it was the key unlocked.

Yeah. Right.

Because of the growing dampness, she double-checked the envelope to make sure it was still securely adhered to the window. Then Kenzie entered the house and, with the flip of two deadbolts, sealed everyone inside.

In about fifteen minutes, she'd start preparing dinner. With Ben now gone and the kids still restricted to a broth diet, it reduced the number of meals to prepare considerably.

Moving to the chair by the living room window, she flipped off the lights and sat in the gloom ushered in by the storm. Fidgeting with her keyring, her thoughts shifted to Shirley. She cursed the old woman for leaving her alone to run the place when she and the kids should be getting out of there. Unfortunately, her only option now was to hunker down and wait for the storm to pass—both figuratively and literally.

The grandfather clock over her shoulder began its chime of five, commanding her to rise and start dinner.

~

Spaghetti with jarred marinara was chosen because of what little effort it took to prepare. Heat the tomato sauce in one pot and boil water in another. Simple enough.

Kenzie leaned on the counter and stirred the bubbling sauce to prevent it from burning.

Outside, the storm brought an unnatural darkness, slicing the remaining daylight hour short. Instead of using the bright overhead fixtures, the kitchen was illuminated by candlelight, but it had nothing to do with trying to set a relaxing atmosphere. With it being so dark outside, having the normal lights on blinded Kenzie to anything beyond the windows. She'd never know if someone was standing right there on the lawn, watching her. Keeping it dim helped prevent the bare windows from acting as a one-way mirror, making Kenzie feel like an animal on display at the zoo.

She stared at the two empty plates reserved for the old women. Instead of setting a third for herself, she'd eat directly out of the pot once the main portions were plated and brought upstairs. Not that she was even hungry.

The steady pounding of rain against the windows was hypnotizing until thunder crashed like cymbals and made her jump. The next lightning flash lit the yard and offered a quick glimpse of the woods. Whether it was her overactive imagination or a simple illusion from the storm's strobe lighting, Kenzie could've sworn the trees had crept slightly closer to the house.

A bubble of spaghetti sauce popped at the surface and splashed her forearm, drawing her attention away from the window. Kenzie hissed and rubbed at the red mark, then stirred the sauce to balance its heat.

She looked back down at the two plates on the tray. It was all wrong. There should be another set for the kids. Lilly loves spaghetti. Tim too, opting for butter and pepper over marinara. And both spooning mounds of grated cheese on top.

It had been nearly three days since Lilly last ate solid food. Two for Tim. Since then, they'd subsided solely on an herbal mixture

Myrna secretly made in her room.

Nothing but that broth. No noodle soup. No nibbling on crackers. Not even Jell-o.

They'd slept around the clock, which should've sped up their recovery time exponentially. Lilly would normally be taking advantage of the down time by reading, yet her book hadn't moved from its spot across the room. And Tim? He should be climbing the walls by now, wanting to go outside and play. With their eyes constantly closed, they were like little moles shunning the sunlight whenever she tried to brighten their room.

Kenzie refused to ignore her intuition any longer, and her paranoia unspooled like a spinning reel of film. Why had she invested so much trust in this Myrna? What did the woman have against giving an aspirin or a spoonful of Nyquil? Why this damn insistence on her herbal remedy and nothing else?

And what type of nurse was she exactly? Obviously one of those holistic types, but what if she was some crackpot who believed in praying away the pain instead of actively seeking medical attention concerning something serious?

Or what if the woman wasn't even a nurse? Until now, Kenzie had trusted Shirley's word that Myrna *was* one, and a good one at that. But what if she didn't have any medical training, and had been fooling them the entire time?

Or if she did have the experience, what if Myrna was out there in the middle of nowhere because she'd been fired for some sort of malpractice or negligence? Something like administering the wrong medication that killed someone. Or failing to notify a doctor when something was wrong? Or smothering a patient to death with a fucking pillow because she was certifiably, bat-shit insane?

Whatever the case, the inciting incident to all of this—coincidence or not—was Lilly first hitting her head against a wood beam, and then on the hard attic floor. And Myrna casually dismissed the entire thing as if dealing with a skinned knee or something.

Kenzie knew she, herself, should've taken her daughter's fall much more seriously. Why hadn't she pressed the issue harder from the get-go? Was it her fear of hospitals, spawned by her mother's illness? How the last thing she ever wanted to imagine was her beautiful children lying in one of those beds, hooked up to tubes and wires, and being told by doctors they discovered something much more serious during a routine test?

Or was it much simpler? Myrna provided free medical care at a time when Kenzie didn't have a pot to piss in?

Or maybe she didn't want to make waves? Offend Myrna by refusing her assessment and, by proxy, Shirley, who might ask them to leave?

Oh, for Christ's sake! It's so far beyond all this now.

The water in the pot boiled over, hissing as it dribbled onto the stove's crimson coil. Kenzie poured some out, then grabbed a stalk of spaghetti, snapped it in two, and dropped the pasta into the bubbling water. In the short time it took to complete the action, she knew what had to be done.

Lilly and Tim had slept long enough. Now they needed nourishment.

Feed a cold, starve a fever. Right? Well, neither kid had a temperature, so it was time to eat.

Maybe if they had some food in their bellies, they'd have the energy to get up and move around a bit. With Paul's impending arrival, she needed the kids active and alert. Not lying in bed, completely vulnerable like two ragdolls.

She snatched a loaf of bread off the counter and brought it over to the toaster.

~

"Baby, wake up."

Tim stirred when Kenzie brushed aside his bangs to check for a temperature. As suspected, his forehead felt normal. With his eyes still sealed, he blindly smiled at her and cleared his throat.

"Come on. Sit up and eat something."

She glanced at Lilly again to see if the girl was still awake.

When Kenzie first entered, she set a plate of toast on the nightstand. Lilly turned away from the commotion, pulling the covers over her head and loudly huffing a warning she didn't want to be bothered. So, Kenzie approached Tim first, giving him a gentle shake.

"Hop up, Lil' Bacon."

He groaned and rose to his elbows. His lids fluttered and tried to open, but the overhead light made him wince and close his eyes before Kenzie could spot his baby blues. The boy slowly wormed his way through the covers until sitting upright, his back pressed against the headboard.

"Atta boy. Now I want you to eat something."

He shook his head. "Myrna said we shouldn't. Not yet."

Kenzie's cheeks grew flushed. "Well, I'm your mother and I say you need to eat. Now, come on." She held the dry toast to his mouth. "Toast. Eat."

Eyes still closed, he sniffed at it and turned away. "Blah."

"Tim. I said. Eat." She pressed the toast against his lips. "Open."

Like a little, blind mole rat, he sniffed again, paused, and finally nibbled.

"Good," Kenzie said, "that's it." And after he swallowed his bite: "Take another."

He did as instructed, groaning his satisfaction, and even took larger portions without being told. Kenzie sighed in relief. The fact he was eating was cause enough for celebration.

Since his stomach had probably shrunk considerably, she fed him only one slice. After swallowing the last of it, he slid back down, and she tucked him in. Although he never opened his eyes, she was satisfied he had something in his belly.

Lilly needed a little extra coaxing, but eventually savored the toast more and more as Kenzie kept it pressed to her lips. Much like her brother, she groaned and rose to one elbow, keeping her eyes closed the entire time while being fed.

The girl had almost devoured her entire slice when Tim began retching in the bed beside her.

TWENTY-THREE

WITH HIS HEAD PIVOTING FORWARD in a sharp, stabbing motion like a cat hacking up a hairball, Tim snapped erect and shot vomit across the room. Although he only consumed a dry slice of lightly browned toast, what erupted was a thick, tarry substance, soiling the entire bedspread and the boy himself.

Kenzie gasped, dropped the sliver of crust she was feeding Lilly, and rushed to her son's side. Tim collapsed back onto the bed in complete exhaustion, beads of sweat popping from his pores and dotting his forehead and upper lip.

Kenzie peeled off the soiled cover and tossed it to the ground, where it landed at Myrna's feet, who was now standing in the open doorway.

The woman stared in shock at the scene taking place, only mumbling, "Wha . . . wha . . . ?"

Ignoring her, Kenzie tended to her son. "It's okay," she told him. "It's okay." She searched for something—a box of Kleenex, a washcloth, a t-shirt—anything within reach to wipe off the inky strands dangling from the corners of his mouth.

Tim slowly exhaled as she cleaned his face using a pair of tube socks from the dresser.

"You're gonna be okay," she told him.

"What have you *done*?" Myrna hissed.

Kenzie glared at the old woman, who was studying the black bile-like substance coating the comforter.

"You did this," Myrna said, holding up the cover. Her initial shock turned to a rage directed solely at Kenzie. "*You* did this!" She tossed the blanket aside, where it landed with a wet splat, then advanced toward the boy's bed. "Move! I gotta see if he's—"

Kenzie met her halfway and blocked her path. "Oh, the fuck you are!" Her fists clenched. She was ready to tear Myrna apart if the woman made a move for either child.

Then Lilly started gagging.

Both women turned to the girl, who was now sitting up, her mouth open and tongue poking in and out with each dry heave.

Myrna quickly retreated to a safer distance until bumping into the dresser by the door, blindly knocking over the candles on top, while her eyes remained glued to the girl.

Kenzie rushed for the trashcan in the corner of the room, dumped its contents, and ran back to her daughter, offering the basket as a puke vessel. "Here-here-here-here!"

Eyes closed, Lilly turned to the sound of her mother's voice and unleashed a thick, hot stream of projectile vomit, blasting Kenzie square in the chest. The black fountain splashed up against her neck and ran down her shirt collar, where the warm liquid coated her flesh and filled her bra.

Once she caught a whiff of Lilly's former stomach contents, Kenzie, herself, gagged and dropped the trash can. She stretched the wet, tepid shirt away from her skin, the action making a nasty suction sound. "Oh, God . . . Oh, God . . ."

Lilly collapsed back to the bed and groaned.

Then an unholy howl echoed from above. "*Noooooooooooo!*"

Kenzie jumped at the sound and spun to face Myrna, whose attention was drawn to the hall.

The scream came from the far side of the house, in the direction of the third-floor bedrooms.

Myrna glanced back at Kenzie and, for the briefest moment, a wide-eyed terror twisted the old woman's face.

With Lucille boldly announcing her presence, Kenzie shivered. But how could the dying woman have heard the commotion from all the way up there? Unless . . .

The ceiling creaked.

Kenzie's eyes shot up.

Unless she had left her room.

Still in the doorway, Myrna craned her neck out into the hall and peered toward the staircase leading to the third floor. Where Kenzie stood, its steps were on the other side of the wall behind her. She stared at its wallpaper as one squeak after another warned her someone was descending the stairs.

Kenzie spun back to Myrna, whose eyes lit up and an insane smile stretched across her face. Then the old woman took a step back, clearing a path into the room.

Kenzie watched. Waited. Her blood ran cold. The entire house fell silent, even the pounding rain and the rumbling thunder slowly muted.

Lucille. It had to be Lucille lurking outside the room. She was the only one left in the house. Which meant the old hag wasn't some bedridden invalid. She could get around. And if so, then Tim's terrifying experience from the other night could've very well been real.

Lilly suddenly groaned, snapping Kenzie from her paralysis. Seeing her suffering child made the storm's ambient noise dial back to normal. Kenzie slid up to the bed, wiped the sweat from the girl's forehead, and held her hand. Feeling Myrna's gaze burning the back of her skull, Kenzie noticed her still standing in the doorway, thankfully, alone.

Lilly whimpered, "I'm sorry, Mom."

"You're gonna be okay, baby. Just relax. I'll get you and your brother all cleaned up." She looked down at the tarry substance coating her upper body and Lilly's covers. It made no sense. They'd only been fed toast, for God's sake! Why was it all *black*? Kenzie turned to check on Tim and found Myrna silently standing over him, her bony hand placed over his heart.

Kenzie bolted up and jabbed her finger at the woman. "I said *no*! Do *not* touch him!"

Myrna quickly retreated, shaking her head.

"What is this?!" Kenzie motioned to the black puke splashed across her chest.

"That's your doing," Myrna said. "Not mine." Her tone was that of a petulant child. "You should've listened to me. I told you not to feed them."

"*This* . . ." again, she pointed at the tarry substance, "is *not* from eating a slice of toast! *This* is from whatever shit you've been making them drink! And this is *not* normal!"

Myrna locked eyes with Kenzie. "You fuckin' idiot. You have no idea how close you came to ruining it all."

Kenzie's jaw unhinged. For a moment, her lips moved but no words came out. "You . . . you're insane! What the fuck are you even talking about? *What* have you been giving them? Tell me! Goddammit!"

Myrna's answer was a simple one. It was only a smile, but one stretched so wide it gave her a lupine appearance.

Kenzie advanced on the old woman. "Get out! Get out and do not step foot in this room again! Do you hear me?!"

The devilish grin remained on Myrna's face while she slowly retreated, gazing at each sleeping child before finally exiting the room.

Kenzie slammed the door in her face and locked it. Adrenaline hammered her heart and an avalanche of thoughts—fast, hard, and picking up speed—began to tumble through her mind.

Oh God-Oh God! What's wrong with my babies! She's been poisoning them! How's Shirley going to react to me yelling at her guest? Really?! That's what you're concerned about? Fuck that! The woman's been poisoning my kids! If Shirley can't see my reason for attacking Myrna, then fuck her too! We gotta get outta here! The kids need a hospital. How am I gonna get 'em there? I'll call an ambulance. But what if the roads are washed out from the storm and they can't get here 'til morning? Maybe they can walk me through what to do to make sure they're okay, until help can arrive. Or if Paul shows up before then, maybe he can take us? And how the hell can I convince him to do that? How am I gonna keep that psycho bitch Myrna out of the kids' room? Where the fuck is Shirley?! Why hasn't she called? What am I gonna do? Fuck! What am I gonna do?!

Kenzie sucked in a breath and pushed back the panic wanting to smother her.

Relax! Relax. That's right. Breeeeaaathhhhe.

First things first . . .

She peeled off her vomit encrusted shirt and tossed it to the ground. A quick check on the children found them fast asleep, yet responsive to her touch. Upon kissing their foreheads, they let off a soft moan and pitiful smile. They seemed okay for now, but she refused to take anything for granted. Not anymore. She would call for a doctor or an ambulance and get washed up while waiting for them to arrive, then lock up the house and let the two bony bitches upstairs fend for themselves. There was still plenty of food available in the house. Myrna could make sandwiches or open a can of soup for all

Kenzie cared.

Speaking of the old woman, if a doctor determined Myrna's broth was the cause of all this, that she was indeed poisoning the kids, Kenzie was going to have the hag thrown in jail.

So much for this place being a haven, huh? Jesus Christ.

The more Kenzie considered the timing of Shirley's departure, the more it seemed she was involved in all this. It was too coincidental. But why would she intentionally put her great grandkids in jeopardy? How could she do that to her own family?

The how and why were too mind boggling, and only served as a distraction from what needed to be done immediately, which was go downstairs to the only working phone in the place and call for help. Unfortunately, in doing so, she'd have to leave the kids unattended.

Just lock the door behind you and go make your call.

After positioning the children on their sides in case they vomited again while asleep, she locked them in, and shoved the keyring deep into her pants pocket.

Making her way down to the front desk, she picked up the phone, pressed the receiver against her ear, and punched nine-one-one. As she silently rehearsed what to tell the dispatcher, a series of loud clicks tattooed from the earpiece. She tapped furiously at the two plastic prongs on the cradle to reset the call, but instead of getting a dial tone, she only heard more clicking.

The howling wind and rain pounded the house, reminding her of what would happen if water seeped into the phone lines.

"Oh, c'mon. C'mon! C'mon!" She jabbed the prongs again and waited for a dial tone that never came. "You gotta be kidding me!"

Going to her room, she retrieved her cell phone and pressed the home key.

The screen remained black. She cursed herself for letting the battery die and plugged it into the wall adapter. With the device now receiving some juice, its screen lit up but only with the image of a battery icon outlined in red. Beyond that, the phone did nothing. *Okay. Give it a few minutes.*

But she knew damn well once it came back up, she'd never get a signal, especially in such a storm.

Shivering, Kenzie caught her reflection in the dresser mirror and slightly blushed. With so much going on, she forgot she was only wearing a bra, having shed the soiled t-shirt upstairs. Originally white, the brassiere was now black and gray from Lilly's vomit. Her chest, neck, and shoulders were slick with the inky substance, diluted by a layer of sweat coating her skin. Leaning closer, Kenzie stared at how awful she looked, like she aged twenty years since only that morning. Her green eyes swam in dark, puffy circles of melted mascara. Chunks of dried vomit clung to the split ends hovering above her shoulders. She picked at the crusty remnants, then shook her head in disgust and grabbed a fresh t-shirt to change into after washing up.

While the phone charged on the dresser, her plan was to get cleaned up and return to the kids' room to wait things out. Bring both the cell and its power adapter—along with a butcher knife for protection—and keep trying to call out while standing watch.

On the way to the bathroom, she unclasped her bra and dropped it to the floor. Once the hot water kicked in at the sink, she lathered up a washcloth, glanced in the mirror, and noticed she'd left the bedroom door open behind her. Instinctively covering her bare breasts with her hands, she considered shutting either the bedroom or bathroom door for privacy . . . then thought modesty can go fuck itself.

She wanted both left open to better hear the kids in case they called for her.

Would you quit wasting time and just wash up?

After her chest and arms were scrubbed clean, she bent down and went to work on lathering her face.

As thunder rolled overhead, the hairs on the back of her neck suddenly shot up. It had nothing to do with the storm's electricity, but an uncanny feeling she wasn't alone in the room anymore.

With soapy water running down her face, Kenzie bolted upright, opened her eyes, and used the mirror to check behind her. Its reflection cast a straight shot through the bedroom doorway and into the shadowy hall. Beyond that was a solid wall of black.

An eerie stillness blanketed the moment, then lightning flashed and revealed the silhouette of someone crouching in the middle of the living room. Once spotted, their head cocked with an audible crack in Kenzie's direction. Then the figure sprung up and forward, dashing for her open bedroom door, their heavy steps pounding across the hardwood floor.

Kenzie gasped and spun around with soap in her eyes. Through burning, blurry vision, she glimpsed someone rushing into her room, ducking behind the bed.

She jumped back, slamming into the bathroom counter with her heart jackhammering in her chest. The shadowy figure was way too tall to be either one of the kids, and too thin to be Paul (assuming he'd just arrived and somehow managed to get inside). Kenzie scrubbed her burning eyes and snatched a towel to wipe her face. With each blink, the world in front of her flickered like a projected film slipping from its sprockets. The towel cleared enough of her vision to be able to grab the t-shirt beside her and throw it on, covering her nakedness.

Keeping her watery, bloodshot eyes locked on the bed, she blindly reached back for something to use as a weapon. Her trembling fingers found a toothbrush and flipped it around, turning it into a pick. Sure, its end was round and plastic but still hard enough to jab at a soft throat or stab deep into an eye or ear.

"Hello?" she asked and immediately felt like a fool for doing so. Someone was crouching on the other side of the bed, hoping to lure her closer. Did she expect a response?

Kenzie stood frozen and listened for any clues as to who it might be.

Myrna?

She swallowed hard.

Or Lucille?

Their brief image, temporarily seared in her mind by the lightning flash, was fading fast. They were thin and, possibly, naked. It had to be one of the old women.

Kenzie cleared her throat, puffed up, and said, "Myrna! Come out from behind there. Now!" Although she attempted an air of authority, tears streamed down her face. She rubbed her burning eyes again.

"Myrna!"

Heavy, rhythmic breathing rose from the far side of the bed. It grew louder and louder until it felt like it would drown out the rain pounding against the window. Kenzie stared ahead and her throat clicked. Terrified of the answer she might receive, she asked . . .

"Lucille?"

The breathing stopped, and the room fell silent.

Likewise, Kenzie's own breath halted in her chest.

Then came a white-hot flash, and an immediate explosion outside the window made Kenzie jump, drop the toothbrush, and scream at the top of her lungs.

TWENTY-FOUR

WHEN LIGHTNING HIT THE TRANSFORMER, it was like being stricken blind. The house lost complete power. Kenzie remained facing the bed and—desperate for some sense of security—quickly backed into the nearest corner, instinctively raising her hands to shield her body. She was terrified something was going to reach out and touch her . . . run its cold, bony fingers along her arm, or across her bare feet. Maybe even gently brush away a strand of hair from her face before caressing her cheek.

As the seconds ticked by, her eyes slowly adjusted. The all-encompassing darkness gradually dissipated like a lifting fog bank and familiar objects began to take shape.

The large, inky mass beside her transformed into the dresser.

Across from it, the open bedroom doorway was now a solid black rectangle.

And the bed? Someone was silently crouching behind it, peeking over at her.

The upper half of their face was an ebony silhouette cast against the white wall. At a passing glance, it could've easily been mistaken for a dark, round pillow. But it moved ever so slightly, cocking its head back and forth before returning upright. It was watching her. Studying her. Its glistening eyes gave off two pinpricks of light that hovered over the comforter's edge and flashed every time it blinked. It reminded Kenzie of the eyeshine of some wild animal in the woods hit by a distant beam of light. Whoever was in the room with her, it sure as hell wasn't either one of the women from upstairs.

Her skin fluttered. Jaw rattled. She found herself turning away from the intruder's glare in the naive notion of "if I can't see you, then you can't see me." Within the gloom, she stared down at the dresser and recognized her cell phone on top.

It became a reminder of what needed to be done: grab the phone and its charger, reach the kids, and (now, more than ever) guard them behind a locked door.

She sucked in a breath and forced herself to look back at the bed.

The figure in silhouette was gone.

Were they just crouching lower, out of sight? Or did they slip under the bed? And were now preparing to spring out from behind the bed skirt, belly-crawl across the floor, and claw their way up her body for a proper face-to-face introduction?

Her stomach soured at a third possible scenario: during the few seconds her head was turned, had they snuck out through the open door and were now making their way upstairs to the kids' room?

She scanned for any sign of the intruder. If she were right about them having already left, then the longer she waited, the closer they'd be to her sleeping children.

Kenzie sprang into action, grabbing the cell phone and yanking its charger out of the wall. Focusing exclusively on the open doorway, she raced across the darkened room.

Just go! Go-go-go-go-go! Get to the kids' roo——!

A cold, clammy hand shot out near the edge of the bed, seizing her ankle and locking her leg in place.

Thrown off balance, she stumbled, clipped her shoulder against the doorframe, and bounced back into the room, landing on her ass. Feeling her leg suddenly released, she tried to scramble to her feet when large spindly hands clamped firmly over her shoulders from behind.

The icy grip forced her back down and a cold breath slid from the back of her neck over to her ear, pimpling the flesh across her entire body.

"*Kill* the children," a deep voice whispered.

With her bulging eyes swimming in their sockets, Kenzie shrieked in terror and wrenched her body free. She flew through the open doorway, across the hall, and into the foyer, where its absolute darkness caused complete disorientation.

With the storm now in full effect, where the hell was all the lightning? Since the last strike knocked out the power, there had been no further bolts streaking the sky, something she desperately needed to help guide her way to the kids' room.

Terror-stricken, she shuffled across the floor to avoid tripping over something and, ironically, did just that when her feet hooked under the carpet runner. As she crumpled forward, her arms shot out to break her fall.

She slammed to the ground and the phone flew from her grasp.

Attempting to recover the device, her trembling hands reached out and raked the polished floorboards. A fresh wave of shivers rippled up her spine at the thought of touching something horrible such as the cold, bare feet of the attacker standing directly above her.

After a few frenzied moments of searching, Kenzie felt the phone's slick surface. Its screen lit at her touch, giving her a start. The battery must have charged enough to give it some life. She flipped it over and aimed it ahead.

Its dim glow only illuminated the immediate foyer. She continued waving the phone back and forth, terrified her attacker might be waiting just outside the screen's reach. When she turned, darkness rushed over her shoulders like rolling waves of black water.

Before she knew what was happening, a cold breath whispered in her ear, "You *must* kill the children."

Too petrified to turn and face her attacker, Kenzie squealed and skittered her way across the floor, toward the steps. Scrambling up to a safer distance, she aimed the phone back down at the lobby, but its light was far too weak to illuminate anything beyond a few stairs.

Trembling uncontrollably, she leaned slightly forward and narrowed her eyes.

A stair creaked below.

Kenzie flinched.

Another squeak. Closer.

A hand reached out of the shadows and planted on the farthest step. Kenzie gaped at the long talons on the raven colored appendage, its flesh glistening as if freshly dipped in a vat of ink. Her pursuer inched forward, and the bald crown of an obsidian skull materialized out of the void.

Kenzie's pulse pounded. It had to be the freak from the woods.

Whoever the hell he was, he'd gotten inside.

Then the bowed head started to rise.

Too terrified to wait and see his face, Kenzie spun and clambered up the stairs on hands and knees, the phone lighting her way.

Making it to the landing, she gasped for breath and barreled down the hall to the kids' room, her free hand spearing her pockets for the keyring to unlock its door.

Lightning finally blasted through the window at the opposite end of the hall. Kenzie looked back.

Striding on all fours, a dark, lanky figure rushed at her, quickly closing the distance.

Kenzie screamed and skidded to a stop at the kids' door. Even with the key at the ready, it took numerous fumbling attempts to gain access. She rushed inside, slammed the door, flipped its lock, and backpedaled to the middle of the room. Using the screen's ghostly light source, she verified the tiny outlines of her children under the covers.

Then came a metallic squeaking that threw her attention back on the door.

The handle slowly raised and lowered.

The son-of-a-bitch was on the other side, trying to get in. Who the fuck was he? Some lunatic dressed in a costume, or wearing Halloween makeup? She continued trying to rationalize it, but knew damn well his stretched torso and those unearthly, elongated limbs blew apart any theory it could be a man in disguise. Yet, it had spoken to her.

Kill the children.

The handle wrenched harder. The door rattled in its jamb.

Before it could burst open, she rushed to the triple dresser.

At first it wouldn't budge. Her bare feet sought traction only to slip repeatedly on the polished floorboards. She stopped, adjusted her stance, and pushed with all her might. It finally lurched forward, knocking over the candle decor and scratching deep gouges in the floor. Once the piece of furniture barred entrance, Kenzie leaned against it to pin it in place.

With her heart pounding in her ears, drowning out all other sounds, it took a few moments to realize the handle had gone still.

The breath rushed from her lungs and she melted to the floor. Although every muscle in her body burned white-hot, she forced herself to rise and search for a weapon, eventually grabbing a brass letter opener off the small desk in the corner. Although both sides of the blade were dull, it was still pointed enough to stab someone. And being made of metal, it had weight to it. It could inflict some real damage.

Before she could even feel remotely safe, the room had to be thoroughly checked to verify they were alone.

With her makeshift knife at the ready, Kenzie lifted each bed skirt and aimed the phone's light underneath, waving it up and down the length of the box spring. The closet was next. She raised the letter opener and jiggled the doorknob with her phone hand.

Okay, just do it!

Kenzie ripped open the door and shoved the light inside, quickly checking all four corners and the shelves above. The small room was practically empty.

Stepping onto the carpeted mat, she searched through what little was on the shelves for a better weapon but found nothing. She shut the closet and returned to the kids who, somehow, even during all the commotion, were still asleep.

Kenzie knelt beside Lilly, cleaned off remnants of black vomit from the girl's chin, and caressed her cheek.

"I'm gonna get us outta here," she whispered on deaf ears. "Everything's gonna be all right. I promise."

The phone beeped twice, and the battery icon appeared on screen. It was nearly drained of the minimal charge it received. Kenzie checked again for a signal and found none. If she couldn't make a call, she damn well better use the last of the battery to search for something to light the candles scattered across the dresser. Rummaging through the desk drawer, she found an old cigarette pack with a matchbook wedged in its cellophane wrapper.

The book only contained three matches.

The first two sparked but didn't ignite, their sulfur heads crumbling over the striking strip. She held her breath, tried the final match, and gushed when it fired up. Two candles were lit, one placed by the door and the other on the nightstand between the beds.

Thunder boomed outside the bedroom window and Kenzie recoiled. The storm was intensifying, the pounding rain sounding more like hail.

She found the nearest outlet and plugged the phone into the charger. Once the power was restored and her battery charged enough, she'd check for a signal. If there was still nothing, she'd be forced to sneak back downstairs and try the landline again.

She shuddered at the thought of having to leave the room, especially with the lunatic who chased her there roaming the house.

What had he whispered to her? Kill the children?

Yeah, if any one of those fuckers come even remotely close to this room, there'll be some killing, all right.

Tim stirred and groaned. Kenzie flew to his side.

"Ma?" he said, his eyes still closed.

"I'm here, baby. You okay?"

He grunted.

"You still feel sick?"

No response.

"Hey. Can you do me a favor and look at me?"

Tim shook his head.

"Please, baby. I wanna see your beautiful baby blues. C'mon, open them up."

His eyes moved back and forth under their lids as if caught in a waking REM state.

"Come on, Timbo. Look at me."

"Can't."

"Yes, you can. Now look at me."

"Nooo." His eyeballs continued swinging like a pendulum.

"Tim. Open your eyes," she commanded.

The boy slowly exhaled and drifted back to sleep.

Disturbed over his wavering consciousness, Kenzie leaned closer and studied him. Sure, he looked peaceful, but she needed to see his eyes.

Lifting one lid, a lump of panic filled her throat so fast it nearly choked her.

His eye was as white as a cue ball. Kenzie tried the other and saw it too was nothing but glistening sclera. She moved the candle on the nightstand closer and pulled up his lid, stretching it tight by the lashes. It wasn't until spotting the faint blue crescent of an iris at the top of his socket that she could breathe again.

His eyes weren't erased, only rolled back in his head, which made the reality of the situation only slightly less unnerving.

A quick check on Lilly yielded the same results.

Kenzie tried to convince herself it was normal. That sleeping as sound as they were made the eyes roll all the way up in their heads. With her lack of medical training, how would she know any different?

Still, it did little to shrink her overwhelming sense of dread.

She sat on the edge of the bed, rocking, staring blankly at the shadowy corner beyond the candle's glow. Waves of self-doubt crashed upon her. Good God, how could she have been so stupid to let it come to this? As their mother—their protector—how could she have failed them so miserably? Did she even deserve to have such beautiful children?

Kenzie looked up and struggled for the words. After a long pause, she whispered, "Please God, I know I haven't prayed to you in forever. That I . . . that I stopped doing it after Mom died. But I'm begging you to please, please look out for my babies. You can punish me all you want for living a less than Christian life, but these kids are innocent. They don't deserve any of this. Please let me get them to a doctor, and please let them both be okay. Let them be perfectly fine and I promise, I'll try to be a better person. A better mother. Okay?"

She waited.

"Please, please, please . . ." She continued repeating the word until the booming thunder cut her off. In her desperation, it was as good of a response as any. She sucked in a breath and smiled. "Okay. I'm gonna take that as a sign you heard me. Thank you. Thank you so much," she said and wiped away tears.

~

She held each child for half an hour—first Lilly, then Tim—and listened to the downpour outside. While cradling them, her eyes remained glued to the bedroom door, now blocked with even more furniture to reinforce her barricade.

An overstuffed chair, too heavy for her to place on top, sat upright in front of the dresser. Aimed in her direction, it reminded her of something the grandmother of a childhood friend once told them during a sleepover. The old woman, suffering from dementia, said an empty chair facing the bed at night invites something to take a seat and watch you sleep. And most likely, it won't be something benevolent like the guardian angel you think is watching over you.

Kenzie shivered at the recollection and was terrified, if her eyes remained closed for even a few seconds, when they reopened, someone—or *something*—would be sitting there. To put her at ease, she threw a large pillow onto the chair. It wasn't much, but at least it blocked an invitation to the empty seat.

~

When Tim grew fussy and pushed her away in his sleep, Kenzie decided it was time to move to the overstuffed chair. She could retire there until daybreak, keep an eye on the kids, and feel if anyone tried to open the bedroom door behind her.

Still clutching the brass letter opener, Kenzie plopped onto the chair, tucked her feet underneath, and hugged the pillow. She gazed at the closed closet door, grimly realizing it was the only place to retreat if anyone broke through the barricade.

It wasn't the two old ladies who were the only threat now.

Kill the children, it said.

Why would . . .

Her eyelids fluttered and drooped.

Why would they even think . . . that . . .

Her head bowed.

That I'd . . .

She sprung erect, trying to fight off her exhaustion. But within minutes, she lost the battle and sleep comforted her like a warm blanket on a cold night.

~

A thump from within the closet stirred her deep slumber.

Somewhere along the borderlands of her unconsciousness, Kenzie heard a long creak echoing across a foggy landscape. When the noise ceased, there was an extended pause of deafening silence. That eerie tranquility was what triggered an alarm in her brain, snapping her awake.

The room was dim. The candles burned low, with frozen pools of wax around their base. Kenzie wiped the sleep from her eyes. She looked around, and stopped at the closet door.

It was wide open.

Springing to her feet, she aimed the letter opener at the closet while checking over her shoulder to confirm both kids were safe in bed and the barricade was still intact.

Lightning flashed at the window and threw her crooked shadow across the opposite wall.

From her current position, she could barely see into the closet, even with its door pushed all the way open, blocking the far corner of the room.

She raised the letter opener and inched forward. Her heart hammered as if trying to smash free. Thunder boomed overhead. Within a few feet of the closet entrance, Kenzie halted and stared into its darkness. Her eyes slowly adjusted to the gloom and saw a square object propped up against the far wall. It looked like the backside of a large picture or painting.

Confused as to how it got there, she knew from checking the closet earlier, it only contained a few knick-knacks on the shelves, and the shag floor mat (its silhouette plainly visible on the ground). Nothing else.

She crept slightly closer and things became terrifyingly clear.

What she had mistaken for a picture or painting was in fact the underside of a trapdoor. And the dark square on the ground? It wasn't the rug, but an open space of cold air leading down into the floor.

She was staring at a secret passageway, a breach into their haven.

Her gut sank.

Then it flat out dropped, when a ghastly voice beside her whispered, "*You must kill the children.*"

A paralyzing fear clamped over Kenzie, allowing only her bulging eyes to shift to the small vertical gap between the hinges in the door jamb.

Behind the open door, someone stood in the murky corner of the room and stared back at her through the sliver of space. "*You have to kill them.*"

An icy chill blasted the marrow in her already trembling bones. Before she could throw her body against the door and pin the intruder in the corner, the door shot forward and cracked her a glancing blow to the temple. The impact sent her reeling along the door's arc until smashing into the opposite jamb.

She bounced back with darkness swarming her vision like a plague of locusts. The room tilted, her knees unhinged, and she hit the floor. Lying dazed, her body was unable to move while her mind screamed for her to get up. Her lids fluttered, vision strobed.

A living shadow crawled out from behind the closet door and passed over her, making its way toward the barricaded entrance.

No. Get up. Kids. My babies.

Something large and heavy scooted across the ground, vibrating the floorboards beneath her. By the time she turned to the commotion, the dresser and other pieces of furniture had been pushed clear of the bedroom door . . . which was now slowly creaking open.

Still unable to rise, Kenzie could only whisper, "Nooo."

Myrna stepped out of the dark hallway and into the candlelit room with a grin that nearly cleaved her face in half. She glanced over at the end of the dresser and said, "Well done, Anthony."

It took every ounce of energy for Kenzie to turn her head to see who Myrna was addressing. Her aching skull pounded, and vision rippled like a pool's reflective surface sprinkled by rain. All she could make out before everything lost focus was a dark figure perched on the dresser like some sort of gargoyle.

"Our prep is almost done," Myrna continued. "Time to bring the lil' piggies to Lucille, so we can start before the moon crests. Now, go. Lucille's waiting."

The blurred shadow nodded, leaped off the dresser, and landed with feline grace between the two beds.

"Noooo!" Kenzie said and struggled to rise. It felt like bags of concrete lay across her back. "Leave 'em . . . alone!"

Myrna glared down at Kenzie in disgust. "And you. The time will come when you're needed, but until then . . ." She stepped forward and kicked Kenzie in the face. The blow caught her at the temple, snapping her head aside. "Sleep now, you fuckin' cunt." Myrna flicked her tongue in mock cunnilingus.

As the old woman cackled hysterically, Kenzie's eyes sealed shut and darkness swept over her.

TWENTY-FIVE

THE POUNDING WAS LIKE HEAVY artillery shelling obliterating her skull. With each passing second, the assault grew louder, closer, more intense. Then it stopped, allowing for a brief, calm silence . . . only to return and destroy that serenity.

As torturous as the noise was, the explosions acted as a beacon within the fogbank of her unconsciousness, guiding Kenzie out of the void.

A thunderclap exploded overhead. One eye snapped open. Kenzie was lying on the floor in the kids' room, a puddle of drool beneath her. The wound caused by Myrna's kick seeped blood into her left socket, where it congealed and scabbed, gluing her lashes together. She slowly rose to an elbow and, while sucking in a sharp breath, pulled apart the crusty eyelid as if cracking a wax seal on an envelope.

Rain pelted the window and the side of the house. Lightning flashed again through the sheer curtains, making her wince.

Once her vision focused, she glanced around the candlelit room. The bedroom door was wide open, the hallway's darkness hovering up to it.

Climbing to her knees, the ground suddenly shifted. She went back down but managed to claw at the bedspread for purchase and avoid face-planting on the floor. After taking a deep breath and moving agonizingly slow, she pulled herself up high enough to peek onto the mattress. Both beds were empty. The kids were gone.

The nightmare was real.

"Tim!" Her scream made the imaginary vice gripping her head twist even tighter. Ignoring the agony, she cried out again for her children. "Lilly! Tim!"

The calls were answered by distant banging.

Her head swung to the open doorway. She fought to focus on the sound, and realized it was coming from downstairs.

The kids! They're signaling me where they are!

Kenzie grabbed a candle for guidance and hissed when its hot wax splashed her hands. She stumbled out of the room and into the hall, the ground tilting on her like the floor of a funhouse.

The knocking was louder once reaching the top of the staircase leading to the ground level. She took a step down, lost her footing, but quickly steadied herself and continued her descent, this time more carefully.

"I'm coming, babies."

The staircase seemed to sway and twist into a double helix, then returned to normal. Her head spun and a wave of bile rose in the back of her throat, burning her windpipe.

Keep moving. They need you. Almost there.

The knocking grew harder. More insistent. And could now be pinpointed to the front door.

As her fugue lifted, her brain jumpstarted and quickly shifted into overdrive. *Were the kids locked outside? Why would they be out there? Maybe it's someone checking on us. Someone who can help. Or someone from the phone company to check the lines. Or the electric company. Or maybe it's Shirley, finally getting her ass home and wondering why everything is locked up. Whoever, whatever the reason, they probably have a working cell phone. I can use it to call the cops, then go find the kids.*

Lightning flashed through the window on the front door and a shadow moved behind its sheer curtain. Kenzie pressed forward, allowing the candle's soft glow to light her way.

"Hello?" she called out and flipped the deadbolts.

She wrenched the handle and swung the door open, then took a step back and was immediately blasted by a cold, damp wind. The gust of air was an icy breath which not only rippled her clothes but extinguished the candle.

Even with darkness attacking from all sides, she could see the silhouette of someone standing on the porch against the strobing storm clouds. Her eyes narrowed to make out a face.

"Hello?" she asked again. The lump in her throat made it hard to speak. "I need help. My kids. They've taken my babies and—"

A familiar, condescending laugh strangled her words in mid-sentence.

"Oh, Kenzie. You dumb bitch. What kinda game are you playing?"

Lightning flashed and revealed Paul rushing at her, his teeth bared, and face twisted with rage. The next thunderclap struck in perfect unison with Paul clamping onto her biceps and slamming her against the wall, pinning her in place.

A groan escaped her trembling lips.

Paul kicked the door shut, threw a hand over her mouth, and pressed himself so close Kenzie could smell the alcohol on his rank breath. During the next lightning flash, he gave the house a quick scan to make sure they were alone, then turned back to her after everything went dark.

"Okay. I'm gonna take my hand away. But I swear to Christ if you scream, you'll regret it." He paused to let the words sink in. "Got it?"

Kenzie nodded and he removed his hand. "The k-k-key," she said. "In the envelope. I taped it to the door. Did you not see—"

"Yeah. Yeah, I got it already. Good girl. But there's also the matter of the money you took. And I ain't leavin' without it."

"But I-I-I put in the note that I'll repay you. Please. I'll send it as soon as—"

"Oh, sure you will. You think I'm that fuckin' stupid?"

Kenzie paused, trying to figure a way out of her current situation, one which could not have happened at a worse possible time. Lilly and Tim were in immediate danger and, ironically, Paul was now the least of her worries. Sure, he was still a threat, but maybe . . . maybe if an alliance could be formed . . .

"I said, do you think I'm stupid?"

"Oh God, no. Course not." *Get outta this! You need to get outta this! Think!*

Lightning strobed for a few seconds, and only then Paul noticed her bruised and bloodied face. He recoiled slightly. "Jesus. What happened to you?"

Think!

"Who fucked up your face?"

Think!!

Then . . .

"I have your money. It's upstairs. But the person that did this," she pointed at her face, "stole it and is holding it and the kids somewhere up there."

"What?"

"It's—it's this old woman who rents a room here. She's crazy. She's been drugging the kids and now she's taken them. She's taken Lilly and Tim. She's taken my babies!"

He studied her to see if she was trying to pull a fast one, but it was impossible to read her in the dark. Instead, he turned and looked at the ascending stairs, then shook his head. "My money. Where is it?!"

"*She* took it."

"Bullshit!"

"I swear she did."

"What're you trying to pull here? Who's really up there?"

The image of the dark, spindly *man* flashed through her mind. Before her hesitation gave her away, she spit out, "Just her. I'm telling you the truth."

"You're saying some old bitch did this to your face?"

"Yes! She sucker punched me!"

He exhaled. "Go. Get. My money." Kenzie knew that tone. Heard it dozens of times before. He was one step away from dishing out a beating.

"I will. But I'll need your help. I know you don't owe me and the kids anything but—"

"You're goddamn right I don't! You stole *my* shit! *My* money!"

THINK!

"I know. I know. And I'm so sorry for all of it. But that woman up there has a lot of money. A lot." She swallowed hard to clear her throat and force out more lies. "And she owes me like . . . like a grand . . . and if you help me get Lilly and Tim back from her, I'll get your money, *plus* give you the money she owes me. I'll hand it right over to you. All of it. How about it?"

He loosened his grip on her arm. "A grand?"

Kenzie nodded. "Yes. And it's all yours if you help. Think of it as interest on what I took. Or compensation for you having to drive all this way to get it back."

He exhaled and looked down.

He's buying it. Kenzie didn't know what the hell she was going to do once they found the kids and her bluff was called on the lack of money. But she'd deal with it then. Right now, she just had to get Lilly and Tim back.

"Does she have any sort of weapon? Like a gun?"

No, just some fuckin' pet freak called Anthony. Kenzie shook her head. "I don't think so."

"You don't *think?!*"

"No. No! Or she would've pulled it on me by now. She might have a knife though."

"A knife I can handle." He released his grip and stepped away. "Okay. Turn on a light for Christ's sake."

"The electricity is out. The storm knocked it out."

Paul shook his head and exhaled. "Shit with you can never be easy, can it?" He pulled out a Bic lighter, fired it up, and waved it close to the floor.

Kenzie welcomed the light and checked her surroundings for any threat other than the one she'd been talking to for the past few minutes.

Paul found the candle she dropped earlier and re-lit it. He waved it around the entryway. "Gotta be something here . . ."

"What are you looking for?" she timidly asked. She wasn't used to questioning his actions.

"Something that'll take out the old broad if she tries to knife us."

Kenzie gushed in relief. "So, you'll help me?"

"Looks like it, don't it? I want my money. Plus that interest."

Any optimism Kenzie felt was quickly replaced by dread over the inevitability Paul was going to lose his shit once finding out he was being played. *The kids. Just get the kids.* She'd reason with him some other way when that time came. "Of course," she said, trying to reassure him. "It's all yours."

He waved the candle behind the check-in desk. "Don't you guys keep like a bat or a golf club back here in case you get robbed?"

Kenzie shook her head.

He shrugged. "Well, don't just stand there, stupid. If you wanna get your kids back, help me find a goddamn weapon." He snatched a globed candle off the counter, lit it, and shoved it at her. "Here. Make yourself useful."

Kenzie took the candle and searched for something within reach, too scared to venture much beyond that. She'd seen firsthand what lurked in the house and debated whether to warn Paul about it.

But if she told him about some sort of maniac (or, hell, a monster), he'd think she was lying or flat out crazy, quickly rescind the offer to help, and return to being another obstacle in getting the kids back.

She peered around the corner and into the living room. Lightning flashed and her eyes fell upon the three-piece fireplace tool set. "Paul! Here!"

He followed her into the dark living room where she grabbed a tool for herself and handed him the next one in line.

He gripped its handle, felt its weight, and sized it up. "Yeah, this might do some damage if someone—" He paused, realizing he was holding the chimney brush and, she, the sharp poker. "Gimme that one," he said, and they exchanged tools.

Kenzie saw the rows of soft, fuzzy bristles and tossed it aside, opting instead for the final tool: the small metal shovel. It wasn't as threatening as the poker but would do more damage than beating someone with a brush.

"All right," Paul said. "Now take me to my money."

She continued debating whether to tell him the true gravity of the situation. Granted, Paul wasn't riding in like some hero to save the day. He couldn't care less about her or the kids. They weren't his. And he had no loyalty to her, especially after she'd stolen from him. His only concern was getting back the key and his money. The former, he said, was already in his pocket, the latter, he thought, waiting upstairs.

She kept up the charade and led the way to the staircase.

At the bottom step, she paused, looked up, and glanced back at Paul. She *had* to warn him. Maybe not about there being a monster per se, but that there *was* something far worse than a crazy old woman up there. At least prepare him. "There's something I gotta tell you."

"What?"

"There's also some sort of animal up there."

"What?" he repeated.

Don't tell him it's a monster. Tell him, "A dog. Or something."

"What do you mean *or something*. Is it a fuckin' dog or not?"

She paused, then, "Yes. But I don't know what kind. Just that it's really big. And fast. Keep an eye out for it."

"A really big dog, huh? Oh, this is getting fuckin' better by the minute. Just get your ass moving, would ya? I want my goddamn money so I can get outta here."

Kenzie climbed the next step and winced when it creaked loudly.

She halted and Paul shoved her forward.

"Keep moving. I'm not telling you again, you hear?"

They continued as thunder rolled ominously overhead. With each step, Kenzie felt the walls closing in. There were threats on both sides of her now, one literally breathing down her neck, the other somewhere up ahead. She wondered what she'd do once Paul found out there was no money. What promise would calm him down long enough so she and the kids could make a run for it?

Make a run for it? Lilly and Tim couldn't stay awake longer than a few minutes. Even if they could run, where would they go? The house was obviously lined with hidden passageways, so there was no safe place inside. And outside, a torrential storm awaited them, along with acres of flooded woods to get lost or die from exposure in.

The only option was to somehow get Paul to drive them out of there. Hell, she and the kids could ride in the bed of his pickup like mangy dogs if it meant leaving the house immediately. There had to be someplace on the way to the highway where they could hop out and seek refuge while he continued on his merry way.

Then again, what were the odds of him doing her any favors once discovering there was no money upstairs?

In hindsight, maybe she should've said the women kept their cash someplace else. Somewhere closer to town, where Paul could drive them to. She remembered passing a rickety storage facility and junkyard on their way in. It didn't seem too farfetched to say the money was stashed in one of the storage units. Once they were there, she could run to the office and beg for help. That's assuming the office would still be open or have an after-hours security guard manning the property.

Then again, if she told him about some storage unit full of cash, he'd forget about finding the kids altogether and just drag her ass out of the house, throw her in his truck and—

The scenario unfolding in her head was cut short when she came across a pair of clawed feet perched on the top railing. Once her brain registered what she was seeing, her heart rammed into her throat.

She gazed in terror as candlelight reflected off the yellowish-orange eyes staring down at her.

Before Kenzie could unleash a scream, the beast sprung up and over her shoulder. She watched in shock and awe as the creature pounced on Paul, kicking his chest with both feet before landing gracefully in a crouching position on the same step where the man stood a second earlier.

Paul hurled down the stairs to certain death while the creature blocked Kenzie from attempting to save him.

Seconds earlier, Paul was checking their rear, looking down the stairs when the massive blow to his chest popped the breath from his lungs. It sent him rocketing back, his feet flying out from under him. The impact was so violent it snuffed out the candle and knocked the fireplace poker from his grasp.

He vanished in the blink of an eye, replaced by a trailing wisp of smoke, the heavy clunk of the poker landing practically at Kenzie's feet.

Paul cleared six steps before landing headfirst on the seventh. His gasp was cut short when his neck snapped, a horrifying crack that churned Kenzie's stomach. His body tumbled down the remaining stairs, limbs wildly flailing like a rag doll, until the darkness completely devoured him below. It all ended with a sickening thud, punctuated by a loud slap of flesh against the hardwood floor. After that, there was no agonizing groan. No whimper for help. Only a deafening silence reserved for the dead.

Kenzie frantically exchanged the small shovel for the fireplace poker at her feet. Having the higher ground to her advantage, she raised the poker and stared down the beast—who, oddly enough, leaned casually on the railing with arms crossed, as if patiently waiting for her to get settled.

Kenzie shook her head in disbelief. This was not someone wearing a costume or make-up. This unearthly horror was real, of flesh and blood. Yet, even within such proximity, she still couldn't clearly distinguish all its features. Its midnight flesh seemed to melt back into the darkness beyond her candle's reach, all except for the demonic eyes nestled under thick angular brows, and the short, cat-like nose with flaring nostrils.

Anthony, Kenzie thought. *Myrna called this* thing *Anthony.*

As if reading her thoughts, he nodded, pushed off the railing, and smiled, showing off a mouthful of razor-sharp teeth. He pointed a clawed finger to the top landing and told her, "Go. Now."

Kenzie's frazzled brain couldn't process what was happening. It was speaking to her. Commanding her.

And why was he letting her go? Why kill Paul, yet spare her?

Before the thing changed its mind, Kenzie seized the moment and slowly backed up the stairs, too terrified to take her eyes off the creature.

At the landing, she spun and sprinted around the corner, into the hall. She ran so hard, so fast, the flame within the globe flickered and nearly extinguished.

She rushed to the kids' room, screamed their names, and, after not finding them, checked her old room across the hall. It was all so pointless. She knew damn well where they were, but had to rule out the possibility they might be hiding in a room familiar to them.

Making her way to the staircase leading to the third floor, Kenzie overshot the turn and stumbled. Completely gassed and fighting for breath, she leaned against the wall. Her head spun and the fireplace poker suddenly felt too heavy to hold.

At the window beside her, raindrops tapped the glass like bony fingertips vying for her attention. She pulled back the curtain to check how bad the property was flooded. When lightning strobed and lit up the lawn, it revealed Paul's F-150 pickup parked along the tree line.

Her heart skipped a beat at the sight of the truck. *There! That's it!* That was their way out.

Of course, the keys were with Paul's corpse, which meant she'd have to return downstairs, where that *Anthony* thing still might be. The idea of backtracking popped her bubble of optimism regarding their escape.

Still, the keys had to be fetched *now*, before his body was hidden within the house.

It'll only take a few minutes if you run like hell. Now, go! Move your ass! Before she was able to take a step, a door opened somewhere above.

Kenzie looked up the stairs.

A faint groan—a *child's* groan—fluttered down. Then another door slammed shut.

My babies! A mother's protective instinct roared to life.

"Tim! Lilly!" she screamed, racing up the steps, forfeiting all element of surprise. She prayed for a response, something that would help lead her to them.

Kenzie hit the landing to the third floor and skidded to a stop. "Tim! Lilly! Where are you?! Please! Please, answer me!" She extended the candle and the ghostly images of four doorways—attic, 3A, 3B, and the linen closet—materialized out of the shadows.

No more bullshit. She was going to take back what was hers. And God help anyone that stood in her way.

Kenzie raced down the hallway, past the attic entrance, toward the first of the two middle doors, both of which were closed.

It was time for her to finally see what was behind them.

TWENTY-SIX

KENZIE PAUSED OUTSIDE MYRNA'S DOOR. Sucking in a deep breath, she turned the knob and pushed. The door creaked open only a foot or so. Raising the fireplace poker, she stared into the band of darkness while working up the courage to step farther inside.

Don't think. Just go. Don't think. Just go.

She sprung forward and kicked the door wide open with enough force it swung back and slammed the wall.

As her candle fought the shadows, Kenzie did a quick check of Myrna's room and found it vacant. She flung open the closet door and jumped back when spotting the large hole in the floor.

It was another trap door, confirming her earlier suspicion the house was honeycombed with hidden passageways.

She cautiously moved closer and lowered the candle into the opening.

The crawlspace was narrow and tight, yet large enough for a thin-framed adult to shimmy through on their belly.

Kenzie yelled inside for the kids and listened. The response was scratching from the far end of the tunnel, followed by a deep grunt.

She bolted up and shuffled back so fast she nearly tripped over her own feet. Raising the brass poker, she got ready to pulverize anything that might pop out of the opening.

Wait. Could it be one of the kids escaping from where they were being held? She took a hesitant step closer. "Tim?!"

Or could it be that Anthony thing tunneling through the house? She gulped. "Lilly?"

The scratching continued only a few moments longer. Then a loud thud from the other side of the wall nearly caused Kenzie to jump out of her skin.

The noise came from Lucille's room.

Rushing into the hallway, she slid to a stop outside Lucille's door. Although it had been previously shut, it was now ajar.

Either someone had been in Lucille's and just left . . . or they had entered, and were now waiting inside for Kenzie, leaving the door open as an invitation to join them.

She placed the ball of her foot against the cold, hard door and pushed. While opening along its wide arc, its hinges creaked and the all too familiar scent of sickness crept out of the room.

Inhaling sharply, Kenzie nearly crumbled. The cheap, floral disinfectant unsuccessfully masking the pungent odors of sweat, piss, shit, and rot burned her throat and reeled her back to a past she hoped never to revisit.

Suddenly, she was back at the hospital. In her mother's room. With the skeletal-like woman shrouded under a bedsheet.

Her knees turned to rubber. She swayed, stumbled, and used the wall for support. Racking sobs erupted from deep in her core.

Don't go there! Not now! Goddammit! Your kids need you!

Letting off a guttural wail, she kicked and elbowed the wall, bringing forth a new pain to overwhelm the old one. Something to keep her distracted and in the present. She pounded the wall again and again, psyching herself up for what needed to be done while battling old demons yearning for a reunion. Once her screams reached a crescendo, she stumbled back, hunched over, and gasped for air. Her feet and arms burned and throbbed.

When Kenzie eventually rose, she wiped away the sweat and tears streaking her face, firmly gripped the fireplace poker, and stepped into the room.

There were mounds of clothes piled two, three, four feet deep along the walls, all cascading to the center of the room where a large darkened canopy bed sat like some ancient artifact unearthed at an excavation site.

Kenzie focused on the bed, its possible occupant hiding behind the cascading fabric. With her jaw rattling, she inched closer until a portion of the mattress became visible through the canopy seam. She extended the candle toward the opening, hoping the action would allow more light in, but it only shifted the shadows and gave the illusion something behind the drapery slid across the bed.

Kenzie wanted to shriek and run away. Instead, she stayed the course and reminded herself of two things. First, if something had been there and moved, it would've caused the mattress to squeak. Second, and more importantly, she didn't have time for shit like this when her children were in danger, terrified and alone somewhere within the godforsaken house.

White-knuckling the poker, she took a tentative step closer and angled the globe downward, as a makeshift flashlight.

The canopy stirred ever so slightly. Kenzie froze, swearing a breath came from the other side.

You made it move. That's all. Now go! She swallowed hard and bound forward, shoving the candle through the opening and pushing aside the fabric to expose the mattress. It took her a moment to register the bed was empty. The rumpled covers were pulled back, exposing an oily indentation of a thin body across the fitted sheet.

Although the room was vacant, the closet still needed checking. She maneuvered the mounds of clothes leading to the open door and, once peering inside, sucked in a breath.

The closet contained another trapdoor, its raised lid rested against the wall. Someone was using the secret passageway to travel from room to room. She thought of the scratching heard earlier followed by the thump. It must have been when the trapdoor swung open and hit the wall.

Then a thought crossed her mind: could all this tunneling lead her to Tim and Lilly?

A loud thud overhead nearly uncorked a scream from her throat. She flinched and looked up just as a second crash hit the ceiling. It sounded like someone had dropped a sack of potatoes on the roof. No. Wait. Not on the roof.

In the attic.

She stepped out of the closet and scanned the ceiling, trying to figure out its geography in relation to the storage space above.

Then a muffled, child-like moan came from somewhere within the murky bedroom.

Kenzie's heart stopped. Her bulging eyes scanned the area. "Lilly?

Tim?"

A large mound of clothes in the corner shifted.

Kenzie lurched back. "L-Lilly?" A pause. "Tim?"

She took a step forward. "It's me. It's Mommy."

The pile moved again. Kenzie halted and waited for confirmation she was speaking to one of her kids.

After a long beat, the response came, but the voice did not belong to any child. "Maaahhhh-mmmeeeeee," it whispered.

The color drained from Kenzie's face.

A clawed hand burst up from the fabric mound. Kenzie screamed and shuffled back.

Long, muscular arms snaked out of the pile. As a dark figure rose, the clothes crumbled away and landed at its taloned feet. Once reaching his full height, Anthony stared down at Kenzie, his mischievous eyes burning bright.

"Mommy?" The creature smiled and extended his obscenely long arms, motioning for a hug.

When Kenzie retreated another step, he lunged forward.

Kenzie spun and rushed for the hall. In her panic, she took the corner too fast and her feet flew out from under her. Bouncing off the ground, her tailbone cracked against the hardwood floor and the candle globe shattered, scattering shards of glass everywhere.

Shrieking in agony through gritted teeth, Kenzie rolled on her side, dropped the fireplace poker, and rubbed her ass with both hands. With the candle extinguished, all went black until lightning strobed like paparazzi flashes outside the hall window. During the burst of light, Kenzie caught sight of the attic entrance and writhed across the floor toward it.

The candle's broken globe crunched under her weight, and she hissed in pain as its glass shards sliced deep into her flesh and muscle.

A floorboard creaked.

Through tear-filled eyes, she pivoted and saw Anthony crouching in Lucille's doorway. He sat cat-like, both hands planted in front of him between legs akimbo, exactly as she had first glimpsed him earlier in the woods during her jog.

The lightning ended and she was stricken blind.

Another creak immediately sounded over her shoulder.

"Go to them," Anthony whispered. "They need mama."

His coaxing was completely unnecessary. Kenzie had already flipped onto her stomach and was now rising to all fours. Broken glass ground into her kneecaps and the soft flesh of her palms. She wailed and pushed off the floor, her bloody hands leading the way while blindly racing for the attic stairs.

The clacking of claws across the hardwood floor shadowed her.

She missed the entry and hit the wall, then traced a trembling hand along its surface until it fell into the open space of the doorway. Kenzie shuffled inside and her bare foot slammed the bottom step with a loud crack. A white-hot pain shot up her leg and throttled the air from her lungs. She folded over and landed on the stairs but still managed to clamber up, leaving a trail of bloody prints in her wake.

Lightning flared through the small attic windows above. A glance behind revealed Anthony scrambling up the stairs after her.

Tapping into the last of her reserve, her legs burst into flight. She rocketed through the entrance and threw the door back, hoping it would hit her pursuer hard enough to knock him down the stairs.

Instead, it simply bounced off Anthony's lean frame and rattled on its hinges as he passed through.

By the storm's pulsing light, Kenzie raced deeper into the attic and sought refuge within a maze of cloaked furniture, wood crates, and cardboard boxes.

Heavy footfalls and scratching followed closely behind.

She dropped to all fours and felt around until her fingertips touched a hanging sheet. Kenzie lifted it and waved back and forth, determining if the space behind it was deep enough to hide in.

A strong bolt of lightning revealed she was kneeling in front of a large dining room table. She quickly slid underneath and let the sheet drop behind her.

Squatting and hugging her bloody knees, Kenzie fought for breath and listened for Anthony.

The hem of the sheet covering the table hovered an inch or so above the ground. Going for a peek under, Kenzie re-positioned herself until kneeling with one cheek pressed against the cold, dusty floor. While waiting for the next lightning burst to see if the coast was clear, she spotted the distinct glow of candlelight coming from the far side of the attic. With her vision blurry from dust, sweat, and tears, she wiped her bloodshot eyes and looked again for confirmation.

Indeed, light was emanating from under the door of the separate storage room across the way. It had to be where the kids were being kept. Where she heard the two loud thuds on the ceiling while down in Lucille's bedroom.

Still face down, ass up, Kenzie scanned the path needed to reach the door and avoid bumping into anything when a cool breeze blew in from behind, causing dust bunnies to roll past her head.

Either someone lifted the sheet behind her before moving on with their search, or they were under the table with her now.

Completely vulnerable in her current position, Kenzie remained frozen and prayed the darkness was all concealing. Only her eyes slid up.

A shadowy face appeared in her periphery, hovering over her shoulder. Anthony maniacally chuckled and planted an arm in front of her, attempting to pin her down.

Kenzie threw back an elbow and lunged forward. Her blow connected, striking cold, leathery flesh. She rolled out from under the table, but clipped her head on a large crate, adding further disorientation to her already near blindness.

When the storm showed mercy and briefly lit up the attic, Kenzie recoiled in terror at what she saw.

She'd backed herself into a corner where the only way out was down the aisle, past the thing waiting under the table. Kenzie glanced at the storage room, then back at Anthony, who looked at the door himself and smiled.

Shit, she thought, realizing she'd just given away her intention.

The kids had to be in there. They *had* to. Myrna must have sent Anthony as a distraction, to keep her busy and stall for time so she and Lucille could do God knows what to her babies.

The thought of any harm coming to them ignited a hard fury, overriding the aching pain in her bruised and battered body. She moved into action, crouching like a runner in a starter position, her head tilted, brow furrowed.

Seeing her sudden burst of strength, Anthony's giddy, fanged smile grew obscenely larger. He bounced and clapped gleefully like a child enthralled by a performance at the circus.

Kenzie did a double take over the odd reaction. He *wanted* her to try to dash past him. It was all some sort of game. A cat toying with a mouse.

Well, fuck you, she thought. *Try to stop me.* Her muscles tightened like compressed springs ready to explode. Her eyes shifted back to the door, focusing on her destination.

Before she made her move, Anthony loudly slapped the ground. "No!" he said, shaking his head in an overly dramatic fashion. His freakishly long index finger wagged in the air, signaling her to wait, then his other hand disappeared behind his back. A moment later, his arm returned and swung out, sliding something heavy and metallic across the floor toward Kenzie.

During the next burst of lightning, she saw his offering: a .38 snub nose revolver.

Ben's pistol split the distance between them.

She shook her head incredulously.

Anthony shrugged and smiled, drool spilling over his lower lip and stretching to the floor.

Kenzie looked back at the revolver. Her eyes darted between the gun, Anthony, and the door with the candlelit glow underneath.

By putting the gun there, was the creature enticing her to move closer? Daring her to approach?

If she did, and moved fast enough, she could grab the pistol, shoot the motherfucker in the face, and finally end this cat and mouse bullshit.

Of course, it could all be a trick. The gun might not even be loaded. Only bait to lure her closer.

Kenzie looked back at the door. Tim and Lilly were in there, she knew it. Every second spent debating whether to make a move put them in further jeopardy.

So, Kenzie lunged for the gun.

Anthony also sprung forward but in the *opposite* direction.

She grabbed the pistol and swung it at the creature, only getting him in her sights long enough for him to disappear around the corner, retreating toward the attic stairwell. She slowly rose to her feet and reserved her aim in his direction in case he reappeared.

The revolver's weight failed to steady her trembling hands. Kenzie flipped the pistol on its side to find the cylinder release. She knew a thing or two about guns from one of her exes, always having such a blast at target practice, shooting beer bottles and cans propped on a log out back at his family's property. She found the textured button, pushed it forward, and the cylinder dropped open. Lightning flashed and reflected off the dotted ring of brass inside. The base of each bullet was smooth and untouched by the gun's firing pin.

It was fully loaded. Six shots to use to protect the kids once finding them. She snapped the cylinder shut, then kept a firm grip on the handle and, as taught, her index finger off the trigger, but resting on its guard.

Why she was given the gun barely crossed her mind. None of it made any sense, but that didn't matter anymore. What did was she finally had a real weapon to protect her family with.

Kenzie turned to the rear of the attic and started for the storage room door.

TWENTY-SEVEN

THERE WAS NO SIGN OF movement under the door.

Kenzie crept closer, placed an ear against it, but heard nothing. After a quick check behind her, she twisted the knob and kicked it open.

Her eyes widened.

The room was lined with various shapes and sizes of black candles, their flames wildly dancing from the wind generated by the swinging door.

Two tables were positioned at the center of the room. Tim lay face up on one, and Lilly, the other.

Both were completely naked.

Kenzie whimpered at the sight or, more so, its implication. "Oh, fuck," she whispered. "Please, no . . . no-no-no-no-no."

The kids appeared to be sleeping peacefully on their backs, their arms at their sides.

The area below each table was crammed with boxes and other cartons, limiting her full view of the room, but what she could plainly see was Myrna lying on the floor, blocking her path to the kids.

Like the children, the woman was naked, only she was on her side with her back to Kenzie. Her legs were bent, one arm stretched above her head, the other hung limply behind her. Both hands were visible and, more importantly, empty. It appeared as if the woman had just collapsed. (One of the heavy thumps Kenzie heard earlier while below?) Like a crimson halo, a small pool of blood slowly crept out from under her head and moved across the floor.

What happened? Did she have a stroke or something? Fell and hit her head?

Who gives a fuck?!

Keeping the gun on Myrna, Kenzie cautiously moved deeper into the room as the door creaked shut behind her. Her eyes darted around, then stopped on a shriveled leg peeking out from behind the far table. Its marbled flesh was lined with bulging varicose veins, much like earthworms burrowing below a milky surface.

It had to belong to Lucille.

Kenzie swallowed hard and tightened her grip on the gun.

With the table blocking most of the woman's upper body, Kenzie retreated a few steps and stealthily approached from the other side.

Lucille was naked and lying on her belly, her face veiled by long, wispy hair. Her spindly arms were outstretched, her arthritically gnarled hands empty. The crone's frail, emaciated body, covered with bulging cancerous growths, looked like a skeleton wrapped in wet tissue paper. It appeared as if she, also, had just collapsed. *There's your second thud.* A small puddle of blood expanded from below the tousled hair concealing her face.

Glancing around the room, Kenzie was dumbstruck. *Okay, I don't know what the hell happened here, but you're wasting time!*

She returned to the other side of the table and stood over her daughter. Lilly had strange soot-like circles around her mouth and nostrils as if caused by smoke inhalation, yet the air in the room was clear, even with all the burning candles. At the table's edge, above the girl's head, a small leatherbound book sat beside a gore-soaked metal plate.

Initially recoiling in disgust, Kenzie took a closer look at the dish and saw it contained what appeared to be two large, pink slugs submerged in a shallow pool of blood. Beside them was an open and bloody straight razor.

"Oh, God. Oh, God." She went to each child and quickly scanned their naked bodies for any incision marks, thankfully finding none.

Kenzie grabbed two dust sheets from below the table and quickly covered each child. She had to get one of them up and walking. There was no way she could carry both kids down three flights of stairs at the same time, and she'd be damned if she had to leave one behind while bringing down the other. No way. These kids weren't leaving her sight ever again.

"Hey! Lilly! C'mon. Wake up!" When the girl didn't respond, Kenzie felt a tightening in her chest. *She's just sleeping. Drugged. She's okay. She's gonna be okay.* She shook her. "Lilly! Come on. Get up!"

Still no response. The only thing keeping Kenzie from having a complete meltdown was she could see the girl was breathing normally. The same with Tim, who also had the strange soot marks around his mouth and nostrils.

"Lilly! Goddammit! Wake up!" She shook the child again, harder, and was on the verge of slapping her when the girl stirred and groaned. "Yeah! That's it, baby! Open your eyes!"

Her lids fluttered and slowly lifted. Lilly winced from the candlelight and rubbed her eyes. Completely bewildered, she gazed at her mother, who sat her up and tightened the sheet around her body.

"It's me. It's Mommy. You're all right." Kenzie noticed the girl staring at the gun in her hand. She lowered it below the table to avoid scaring the child any further. "It's okay, honey. You're safe."

Lilly glanced over at Tim, then looked back at her mother in a wide-eyed panic. Kenzie nodded before the girl could speak. "I know. I'll check on him. You just get up, okay? I need you to walk. Can you do that?"

Lilly nodded and Kenzie gushed. Even if Tim didn't wake, she could carry him down with her daughter by her side. Then, once at ground level, they could search Paul for the keys, take his truck, and finally get out of that goddamn house.

Thankfully, Tim awoke at his mother's touch. Rising on one elbow, he grunted and opened his blue eyes. Kenzie welled up with tears.

"Tim," she said. His focus remained solely on his sister. "Tim!" She stepped around, blocking his view of Lilly. "Hey. Mommy needs you to get up." She pulled the sheet tighter around his small frame. "Do you think you can walk?" Without having to be asked twice, he slid to the edge of the table. "Atta boy!"

A guttural groan made Kenzie jump and almost drop the revolver.

Across the room, Myrna was on her stomach, struggling to rise. The old woman murmured something, the garbled words bubbling out as if spoken with a mouth full of water.

While Lilly helped Tim off the table, Kenzie aimed the gun at the woman. "Stay down!" she commanded.

Myrna's head snapped up with a frenzied look twisting her face. Like the children, she had soot marks around her nostrils and lips. Red ribbons of drool stretched from her blackened mouth and ran onto her sagging breasts. The woman attempted to speak again, but what came out was only a gurgling gibberish. She paused and dipped her fingers into her mouth, then felt around and winced. When she withdrew her hand and saw it coated in blood, her eyes exploded with hysteria.

Myrna attempted to speak a third time, but her bloody mouth was reduced to a grotesquely obscene, puckering orifice.

Even by candlelight, Kenzie could see the woman's mouth appeared all wrong. It was vacant. Void of a—

Kenzie spun back to the straight razor and two fleshy slugs served up on the bloody platter. Before she could react in disgust, a bony, palsied hand shot up and slammed onto the table, clipping the edge of the metal dish and flinging the severed tongues across the room, where they landed with a wet splat.

Using the table for support, Lucille groaned and struggled to pull herself to her feet.

Tim and Lilly shrieked in terror. "Mommy!" "No!" "They're coming!" The children stared in wide-eyed horror at the hags.

Kenzie screamed for the kids to get behind her. Tim and Lilly dashed over and clung to her waist so hard and fast they nearly knocked her down. She whipped the gun back and forth at the two women while slowly retreating for the exit.

Lucille's face finally appeared over the table's horizon, forcing Kenzie to stop and stare out of morbid curiosity. The crone's silky gray hair was fine and sparse on top, making her leathery skull even more pronounced. Under her bony brow, deep set sockets housed one ghostly cataract eye while a tumorous growth erupted out of the other like a pus-covered cauliflower floret. An outgrowth of lumpy masses sprouted across her face, neck, and upper body like mushrooms on a rotting log. As the woman continued to pull herself up, she revealed blackened nostrils and a tongueless, soot-covered mouth. Blood spilled over her lower lip as she tried to speak.

Why in God's name had these women mutilated themselves by cutting out their own tongues? Maybe the batshit crazy look in their eyes had something to do with it.

With bony arms extended, they trudged forward and clawed for

Kenzie.

She shoved both kids behind her, shielding them from the approaching horror.

"Open the door! Open the door!" she told them while trying to remain focused on the crazed hags.

The pistol swung like a pendulum between the women.

Tim struggled with the doorknob, wrenching it back and forth.

"Open it, dammit!" Kenzie yelled over her shoulder.

"I can't. It's locked!"

Lilly pushed him aside. "Let me try!"

The old women stared bug-eyed at the children attempting to escape and frantically shook their heads.

Tim saw them eyeing him and threw his arms back around his mother's waist. "Mom! No! Don't let them touch me there again! Please! It hurt!"

Kenzie looked down at Tim. "Wha—?" she asked incredulously. It took a few tries for her to complete the sentence. "W-w-what did you say?"

Tears streamed down his face. "I'm sorry. I tried to stop them. I did. But they held me down and . . ." Unable to meet her gaze, the boy lowered his head.

Kenzie thumbed back the hammer on the revolver. Its loud snap drew the women's attention off the children and back to her. "You sick fucks!" she said between clenched teeth. "Stop! Right now! Or I swear to Christ, I'll—I'll . . ."

But Lucille and Myrna continued creeping forward, drooling blood, their gnarled hands clawing for the family.

"Lilly!" Kenzie screamed over her shoulder. "Get that damn door open!"

"Can't! It's locked! It's locked! It's locked!"

Kenzie turned to help. "Let me try!" She moved for the door, keeping the gun trained on the women.

Lilly stepped aside, then her eyes widened, and she pointed past her mother. "Ma! No! Please don't let them touch us there again!"

Kenzie stared at her daughter and whimpered over the confirmation of a parent's worst fear. *Oh, God! Why? Why?!*

Before she could try the doorknob herself, Tim screamed, "Ma! Look out!"

When Kenzie spun and saw the women within reach, grabbing for the gun, their bony fingers and long nails clacking against its barrel, a blinding rage ignited within her.

There was no goddamn way in hell they were going to touch her children again.

She screamed and pulled the trigger.

Twice.

The first bullet punched a hole through the bridge of Lucille's nose and sprayed a pink mist out the back of her head. The frail woman dropped instantly, most likely dead before reaching the floor.

The second slug tore through Myrna's wrinkled neck, and a gurgling hiss escaped her throat. She threw her hands up over the wound, then stumbled back, bounced off a table, and collapsed. She floundered on the ground for a few moments, before finally going still.

Kenzie trembled uncontrollably. Her knees unhinged, dropping her to all fours, and she threw up. The acrid smell of gunpowder filled the room and burned her nostrils while stomach acid burned her throat. After spitting a few times to get rid of the vile taste, she wiped her mouth with the back of her hand and groaned.

When she glanced back up, Tim stood between the two dead women, looking from one to the other as their pooling blood closed in on his bare feet.

"Tim! What the fu—" she caught herself. "Get away from them! Now!"

A click and a long creak sounded over her shoulder. She saw Lilly standing in the open doorway and shook her head in disbelief. "How? I thought—I thought it was locked."

Lilly waved them over. "Come on. Let's go."

Tim walked past his kneeling mother and grabbed a candle on his way out of the room. Lilly did the same.

Still gripping the pistol, Kenzie bolted up. "Wa-wait! Wait! Get back here." She rushed ahead of both kids and scanned the dark attic. "It's not safe out here. There's something else—"

"It's okay," Lilly said. "We're safe now. You saved us." She slowly closed the storage room door behind her, sealing the corpses of the two old women in their makeshift tomb.

Kenzie's mind was ablaze, completely baffled at how calm the kids were acting. It must be shock. Or they're still doped up on whatever drugs they'd been given. "Get over here and stay next to me. Don't leave my side. Don't wander ahead. Got it."

Tim and Lilly exchanged a glance before joining their mother.

Kenzie kept the gun raised, its barrel guiding them as they slowly maneuvered through the attic by way of candlelight. Her bulging, bloodshot eyes searched in every direction. She prayed Anthony was long gone and not waiting for an opportunity to strike. If he planned to attack, she took slight comfort knowing the gun still had four bullets, which could move much faster than he ever could. At least she hoped so.

Okay! Get downstairs. Find the truck keys. And get the hell out.

When they hit the top landing to the attic stairs, Kenzie paused and gazed down the cavernous passage. She aimed the gun into it, breathed deeply, and stepped forward to lead the way.

Tim and Lilly stayed put. Feeling them let go, she turned back to the kids. "It's okay. We gotta go down and get the truck ke—"

A blinding light blasted up from the stairwell.

Kenzie gave a hissing intake of breath and pointed the gun down the stairs.

"No. Wait," Tim said. He gently laid his hand on top of her wrist, pulling it down enough to prevent her from taking proper aim.

"Kenzie?" a voice called up from the base of the stairs. It was Shirley. The woman was shining a flashlight up at them.

No longer trusting anyone, Kenzie kept a firm grip on the pistol, raised her arm, and took aim.

"Heavens to Betsy, child! What are you doing with a *gun*? Could you please not point it at me?" She aimed the flashlight at her own face so Kenzie could see she wasn't a threat.

Was Shirley one of them? Was she a part of this whole damn thing? "Where the hell have you been?!" Kenzie screamed.

"I told you, I was at my . . ." She paused, shook her head, and exhaled. "We can talk about all that later. I'd like to know what's going on here." Shirley looked past Kenzie. "Children? Are you all right?"

Lilly and Tim remained silent. Kenzie glanced back at them. She honestly had no idea how they'd respond. *Were* they okay? Were they in shock? Were they going to need decades of therapy to deal with all this?

The kids nodded at Shirley. Then Lilly said, "You'll be rewarded for your loyalty, sister."

Kenzie did a double take at her daughter and was about to ask what the hell she was talking about, when Shirley gushed out loud at the bottom of the stairs. There was blubbering followed by a squeal of excitement. Kenzie watched the old woman drop to her knees, place the flashlight on the ground, and raise her hands in the air as if about to scream Hallelujah! Swaying back and forth, she chanted some sort of gibberish.

Kenzie turned back to the children and her eyes widened. Both were pressed up against her, invading her private space. She moved back to see their faces and wound up teetering on the top step. "What are you talking about?" she asked Lilly. "Why did you say that?"

Lilly exchanged another glance with Tim.

"Lilly?"

No response.

"Lilly, I'm talking to you!"

"No. You're not," the girl said, smiling. "Not anymore."

Kenzie shook her head in confusion. Had everyone gone insane? She turned to Tim, hoping he could provide some sort of answer or, at the very least, act somewhat normal.

But the boy only stared up at her in silence.

Kenzie noticed his left hand was moving, his ring finger and thumb tapping in beats of three.

"Why are you doing that?" she asked her son.

Tim smiled.

Kenzie pointed at his hand. "Stop that."

He didn't. In fact, his finger and thumb went into overdrive.

"Stop it!"

Lilly laughed. But the sound didn't belong to her. To Kenzie, it wasn't her daughter's laugh, the one that always brought her such joy, such as when blowing raspberries on the girl's belly, making her giggle uncontrollably.

Kenzie felt lightheaded. "Stop it!" A ball of dread in her gut was cracking open. "Stop it!" Something cold and nauseating leaking out. "Stop it!" Working its way up her chest. "Stop it!" Until it coiled around her pounding heart and constricted. "Stop it!"

"Stop it!!"

"Stop it!!!"

The kids lunged at her like wild beasts and pushed as hard as their tiny bodies allowed.

Already off balance, Kenzie flew back and tumbled down the stairs before her world went black.

~

A light slowly rose out of the darkness that brought forth a blinding pain.

Kenzie lay in the hallway at the base of the attic stairs with a flashlight blasting her face. She winced and tried to climb to her feet, but her body refused to move.

Tim slid the light from her eyes and bounced its beam off the polished floor.

Kenzie looked up and saw the kids standing over her. A euphoric Shirley knelt between them, kissing their tiny hands while chanting something alien.

The children seemed oblivious to the old woman's antics, instead choosing to study Kenzie as if she were an abstract piece of art, tilting their heads one way, then the other. Kenzie noticed Tim's left hand was twitching that nervous tick.

"Wanna let the cunt live?" the boy asked Lilly.

Shirley's smacking grew louder, more intense. It became grossly obscene when she started grunting while tonguing in between their tiny fingers. And yet, they continued ignoring her.

While Lilly still pondered Tim's question, a shadow with fiery eyes slinked up beside the girl and rubbed its cheek against her hip. Lilly placed a hand on Anthony's skull and gave him a welcoming scratch behind a pointed ear. The beast's eyes glowed and rolled up in ecstasy.

Lilly finally answered, "Why not? Are we so merciless? Besides, we've all smelled how useless her body is. Why take what little remains?" She reached down and caressed Shirley's cheek indifferently. "Shame, really. It would've made things so much easier for us all."

Shirley stared up, quickly nodded at Lilly, and jutted her lower lip in disappointment at Kenzie.

Then the two old souls, wearing the flesh of children, along with their obedient familiar and groveling servant, stepped over Kenzie and made their way to the descending staircase.

"Nooooo . . ." Kenzie whispered. "Wait."

But they were already gone.

Broken, Kenzie exhaled, turned away, and closed her eyes.

TWENTY-EIGHT

GASPING AWAKE, KENZIE REACHED FOR her splitting skull, but the handcuff snapped her arm back to the bed. She winced and tried with the other. It too was cuffed to the metal bed rail.

Kenzie groaned, glanced around the hospital room, and, assuming she was alone, was startled by the elderly man seated in the far corner, staring back at her. He wore a police uniform. A cup of coffee hovered below his lower lip as if he were about to take a sip. Instead, he slowly rose, dropped a neatly folded newspaper onto his seat, and set the coffee on a nearby cart. After grabbing his belt, he sucked in a breath and hiked up his pants as far as his pot belly allowed.

Kenzie silently watched him mosey over to her bedside.

"Afternoon, ma'am," the man said. "I'm Sheriff Dwayne Clarkson. Do you know where you are?"

Kenzie shrugged. "Um . . . a hospital?" She yanked on the cuffs again, grating metal against metal.

Clarkson grimaced at the nerve-wracking sound.

"Why am I wearing these?" she said, continuing her struggle.

Clarkson patiently waited for her to stop before answering. It was pointless to try to talk over such racket. "Just a precaution. Until I get some answers."

"Where are my chil . . . dren?" She struggled with the final word, suddenly remembering the answer.

Clarkson took note of her pause. "That's what we're trying to figure out."

Kenzie sat up the best she could, given the restraints. "They're not at the house?"

"No, ma'am. But there are three bodies there that need some explaining for. One looks like he took a nasty spill down a flight of stairs. And then there's the two in the attic with gunshot wounds." He pointed his double chin at Kenzie's ink-stained fingers. "We needed your prints to see if they're a match on the gun we found. Since your hands already tested positive for gunpowder residue, I'm willing to bet they will."

"I had to," Kenzie whispered.

He leaned closer. "Do what now?"

"They were drugging them. T-t-touching them. They must've brainwashed them or maybe it was hypnosis. Whatever it was, it made them act like the old women."

Clarkson shook his head in confusion. "Ma'am?"

Kenzie didn't respond, only stared blankly past him, remembering the look in Lilly and Tim's eyes before they pushed her down the stairs. So vacant. Cold. Spiteful. They might have looked like her children, but . . .

The sheriff exhaled. "Okay, Ma'am. How 'bout you start at the beginning?" He dragged his chair over and pulled out a tattered pad and golf pencil from his breast pocket. "How 'bout you tell me what happened up there?"

Kenzie looked away and exhaled, deflating to half her already tiny size. She squeezed her puffy eyes shut and immediately saw Myrna and Lucille coming at her in the attic. The image was burned on her lids, something that would haunt her for the rest of her life.

What if . . . what if it wasn't hypnosis or brainwashing?

If she fought off an actual fucking monster to reach her children, then why was it so hard for her mind to accept what she saw and felt in her heart?

At the time, while in that storage room, what she had mistaken for bloodthirsty insanity on the women's faces might've been something else entirely. What if it wasn't rage or malevolence, but . . . confusion? Terror?

Her eyes snapped open and were filled with so much horror it caused Clarkson's spine to stiffen.

Even with a gun pointed at them, they were rushing toward me for comfort. For answers. For a mother's security.

Kill the children.

It made no sense at the time. But they'd played her perfectly from the very start. Beginning with Shirley's invitation to visit.

Her beautiful babies were gone. Even if the authorities tracked down Shirley and brought them all back, it wouldn't matter. Tim and Lilly . . . they . . . *they* were gone.

And realizing such finality was accomplished by her own hands, Kenzie sunk even deeper into the mattress and wept.

~

Her flesh was a thing of beauty. Firm. Unblemished. Pure.

Lucille, safely cocooned in the skin of little Lilly, sat in the passenger seat of Shirley's Cadillac while it plowed down the interstate. She stared in awe at her tiny hand, turning it over and flexing her fingers. There was no stabbing pain from arthritic joints or swollen knuckles.

The constant ache residing deep in her bones for decades was gone. The fogginess from cataracts, dissipated. The world outside the windshield was now bright and crystal clear. And the warm sun never felt so good across her smooth skin.

She sensed being watched and immediately turned to Shirley, who nervously smiled and darted her eyes back to the road, keeping her head slightly bowed as a show of respect.

Lucille stared at the old woman, studying her profile. Her thick, gelatinous arms jiggled and bounced with every bump in the road. The drooping flesh under her chin looked more like a turkey's wattle with each passing year. The puffy eye bags. Thinning hair. Spider veins and liver spots. Her sagging breasts resting on the much larger sack of fat that bubbled at her waistline, amplified two-fold while being seated.

The young girl looked down at her own body. At the thin, small frame which would soon blossom. She placed her palm over her flat, firm belly and breathed deeply. Her lungs were clear. The ghastly wheeze gone.

A boy giggled over her shoulder.

Lucille rotated and stared into the backseat.

Returning true to form, Myrna wore the boy, something she'd have to get used to again when it came to her mannerisms. The child sat beside the large wicker basket with one arm stuck deep inside. Its lid was raised only a few inches, enough to expose a strip of darkness where two yellowish-orange eyes flashed bright before dropping out of sight. As the boy pet the thing inside, he stared out the window, awestruck at the endless miles of shopping centers and restaurants running parallel to the highway.

Lucille faced forward and propped her tiny bare feet on the glovebox. Once again, she inspected Shirley and pitied her. She could already smell the rot spreading throughout the old woman, but the scent was not nearly as potent as the sickness they'd detected lying dormant in her granddaughter.

Kenzie's cancer was still asleep, but on the verge of waking in a rage, which would quickly ravage her body as it did to her mother. It was disappointing to lose the vessel. Things would be much less conspicuous keeping mother and children together.

As a result, Shirley's opportunity for extension had passed. When her time came, they'd let her go to the earth, then find her replacement, as they had for their keeper before her. But, overall, the old woman had done well in her servitude.

As if sensing the girl's approval, Shirley peered over and smiled.

Lucille did not return the gesture. Instead, she slid on a pair of children's sunglasses taken from the front console, nestled back, and inhaled deeply, testing her lungs once again.

They'd soon be at the reunion, and she was excited to see the new faces of her family, as well as to show off her own. Until then, she would not sleep, having done so for far too long.

Lucille stared out the window and took in both scenery and sunlight . . . all while imagining the great opportunities *this* life was going to bring.

AUTHOR BIO

Matt Kurtz is a former feature film director and screenwriter turned novelist. He has a three-volume collection of short stories entitled *Monkey's Box of Horrors*, *Monkey's Bucket of Horrors*, and (the even more ridiculously titled) *Monkey's Butcher Block of Horrors*.

His first novel, *Kinfolk*, a horror/action thriller, was published by Grindhouse Press in late 2018.

To read more about him and his work (or to just say "hi"), visit www.MattKurtzWrites.com or find him on Twitter at @MattKurtzWrites.

Other Grindhouse Press Titles

Printed in Great Britain
by Amazon

84722836R00116